Shaky Pictures of Vanished Faces

D. Matthew Urban

Cursed Morsels Press

Critical Praise for D. Matthew Urban

"Puncturing the veneer of normalcy, D. Matthew Urban's *Shaky Pictures of Vanished Faces* undermines traditional values with its unique and complex expressions of desire. No one is safe in these delicately written, yet violent stories. Voices of insects, aliens, cultists, parasites, and other incomprehensible beings invite us to see community, family, and home through an uncanny lens."

- Joe Koch, author of *The Wingspan of Severed Hands*

"*Shaky Pictures of Vanished Faces* collects D. Matthew Urban's most wonderfully vivid and strange short fiction. The prose is brilliant throughout, the stories smart, disquieting, and often darkly humorous. Much recommended!"

- Christi Nogle, author of the Bram Stoker Award-winning first novel *Beulah*

"The stories collected in *Shaky Pictures of Vanished Faces* read like nightmare glimpses of and uneasy prayers to the hidden maw of the weird just behind our world. Driven by the strange engines of impossible ordeals, family rituals, and the inescapable replacement of the everyday by the strange and, at times, playfully grotesque, D. Matthew Urban's fiction reveals, deceives, and delights through new dimensions of horror."

- Gordon B. White, finalist for the Shirley Jackson and Bram Stoker Awards

"Urban's stories are the horrors you can't quite grasp, slipping and slithering just out of mind's reach. They lurk in corners, crawl over your flesh, scratch at the back of your subconscious months later. *Shaky Pictures of Vanished Faces* is a showcase of skill, restraint, and unexpectedly playful grotesquerie."

- J.A.W. McCarthy, Bram Stoker Award and Shirley Jackson Award finalist, author of *Sleep Alone*

Contents

Notice on Content Warnings

Content warnings for each story are available at the back of the book.

Dedication

For Celina

A beam falls atrandom and you disappear
Like a fist whenyou open your hand
      - The Mekons, "Flitcraft"

We call you, say:go down
It is not
            in the world
                    as it seems.
      - Charles Olson, "A Spring Song for Cagli"

The Consultant's Hand

Your new office lies at the end of a long, bright hallway. As I escort you there, I sense your unease mounting. Your eyes dart left and right, peering through doorway after doorway into rooms where desks sit unoccupied, lecterns stand empty, spotless chalkboards glow like virgin meadows lit by fluorescent suns. No words on the chalkboards, no books on the shelves. No students, no instructors. Only stillness and emptiness and the lights' perpetual hum.

"Hasn't the semester started?" you say. "Aren't classes in session?"

"Yes, since two weeks ago," I say. "Which, of course, made us all the more anxious to fill the position as quickly as possible. I can't tell you how grateful we are that you were able to join us on such short notice. After Professor Tryon's abrupt departure, we thought we might have to cancel her classes. Reshuffle enrollments, refund tuition. An administrative nightmare."

Our footsteps echo along the speckled tile, coming back to us from the end of the hallway as if we were there already, walking toward ourselves. I read the questions scrawled in your darting eyes, fear's unmistakable signature in your quivering mouth. I smile and give you a reassuring pat on the shoulder. There is nothing to be afraid of. Soon, you will know all.

If you'd joined us only a year ago, instead of peace and tranquility you'd have found chaos, the typical disarray of an understaffed humanities department at a small and unprestigious public college. Professors harried to madness by budget cuts, sleep-deprived students rushing from class to job to home to job to class, adjuncts staring hollow-eyed into the void of no future ... no offense, of course! And trapped in that madhouse, swirling in that whirlpool, you would have found me, an assistant professor struggling to keep my grip on the lowest rung of the golden ladder. I was the second-to-last non-contingent hire before the university began cutting the department's tenure lines. The last was Professor Tryon.

We've reached your office. I hand you the key. "Welcome to the department!" I say.

...

"Hmm. Are you sure it won't open? Try again. Try jiggling the knob."

...

Well, that old fool in the department office must have given me the wrong key. Never mind, I know where all the keys are kept. Come with me.

Yes, in those days I was a mere assistant professor. Not as lowly as some—how do you adjuncts survive, I wonder?—but hardly an exalted personage. Hardly the head of the department. How did I rise so far in so short a time, when the wheels of academia turn as slowly as dreams revolving in a dead god's brain? Simple. I seized the initiative. I saw a chance, and I took it.

I recall last year's first departmental meeting as clearly as my daughter's darling face. Needless to say, I had no idea what that hour would bring. None of us did, except old Professor Casimir, the department head at the time. The rest of us expected nothing but the usual tedious bickering over course loads and committee appointments. I remember Professor Tryon nudging my shoulder as she took the seat next to mine at the long table in the seminar room—that seminar room there, the one we're passing now. "Are you ready to be … enraptured?" she whispered, rolling her eyes toward the head of the table where Professor Casimir sat, rehearsing his opening remarks under his breath.

I can almost hear those words now, Professor Tryon's whisper taking shape from the hum of the fluorescent lights. *Are you ready to be enraptured?*

Professor Casimir's remarks began with the standard announcement of catastrophe. More budget cuts brewing, state legislators huddled like warlocks around a cauldron conjuring famine. The standard phrases followed—"tighten our belts," "do more with less." Next to me, Professor Tryon let out an almost-silent groan. I felt her breath, soft and warm on my cheek. My mind wandered from the meeting.

When I refocused a few moments later, Professor Casimir was saying, "The administration realizes that previous reductions have left our resources strained, and that the expected cuts will make it even more difficult for us to fulfill our educational mission. They have generously decided to assist us by ..."

"Reducing their own salaries?" someone said from the far end of the room, their voice disguised with a cough. I hid my smile behind my hand. Professor Tryon chuckled.

"... by offering the services of a consultant," Professor Casimir continued. "A consultant who specializes in this sort of thing."

Behind me, the door of the seminar room swung open. A chilly draft from the hallway raised goosebumps on the back of my neck.

"And here he is!" Professor Casimir said.

The consultant strode to the head of the table, moving as if wrapped in a holy nimbus of certainty. His face was sharp and spare, his dark suit perfectly tailored. Absolute confidence glared from the round lenses of his wire-rimmed glasses.

"You may expect I've come to teach you how to squeeze blood from a stone," he said. "How to *do more with less*." Repeating the hackneyed phrase, the consultant shot a scornful glance at Professor Casimir over the tops of his glittering lenses. The department head seemed to shrivel in shame under that gaze, to wither before our eyes.

"Well," the consultant said, "I'm not here to teach you that. I'm not here to teach you anything. You're the teachers, not me. You're the heroes, and I am your humble servant. I'm here to help you realize what you already know. There's no need to squeeze blood from a stone, because stone itself is nothing but blood. There's no need to do more with less, because you can do everything with nothing."

Yes, this way, down the stairs. All the way down to the bottom of things. Why they keep the keys in the basement I'll never know.

Except for Professor Casimir, who'd long learned to dance to whatever tune the administration cared to whistle, we were all pretty skeptical of the consultant at first. I remember Professor Tryon imitating his oily smirk and preacher's voice over dinner with me and my daughter, leaving us howling with laughter. My daughter loved Professor Tryon. Almost as much as ... well, never mind.

But you already realized I was in love with Professor Tryon, didn't you? Of course you did. The bit about her breath on my cheek was something of a giveaway. And after all, you're a literature teacher. Interpretation is your business, your passion. You love to unravel clues. You can't resist a puzzle. Any more than Professor Tryon could.

Anyway, we laughed and made fun and were skeptical. *Just a bunch of hot air, another snake oil salesman peddling the same old austerity bullshit.* So we thought, at first.

Until the trainings started.

We assembled for the first training in the same seminar room where the consultant had given his spiel. The chair at the head of the table sat empty. I had a slight headache that made the glare of the fluorescent lights seem harsher than usual, their hum more piercing. In the seat next to me, Professor Tryon rolled her eyes and moaned with boredom. That breath on my cheek again. My head spun. I closed my eyes.

When I opened them, the consultant was sitting at the head of the table, smiling his holy smile. A book lay open in front of him, a thick old hardcover with yellowed pages. *Middlemarch*, maybe, or *The Mysteries of Udolpho*. He raised a spread hand, let it hover palm-down above the tome.

"You're all scholars, lovers of the humanities," he said. "You've all been accustomed to regard a book as something sacred. When you see your students hunched over their phones, watching little videos and giggling at shitposts instead of relishing the masterpieces of literature, your tender hearts ache with pity. *I have to save them*, you think. *I have to give them an education.*"

Above the book, his hand began to quiver. My headache contracted into a single point of agony like a drill boring out from inside my brain. The glaring lights flashed on his fingernails. The hum rose to a banshee wail.

"In the back of your mind, though," he said, "you know it's only a matter of time. Books, literature, the humanities, all of it—it's fading. Draining out of the world like oil out of a cracked pipeline. What you've spent your life on, all the passions of your heart… it's all nothing. You know this. In the back of your mind. At the bottom of your soul."

His hand shook and flailed as if he were having a seizure, but his face was totally calm, his voice smooth and placid. I looked into his eyes, blazing with holy truth behind lenses that reflected the fluorescent lights' empty glow, and I knew he was right. It was all nothing. My life, my years of work, for nothing.

"That is what I've come to help you realize," he said. "And that is what you will help your students realize. Because it's not only books that are fading. Books are like the first leaf of autumn, whirled down beautifully in a gentle breeze. And what comes after autumn? You know, don't you, what kind of storm is on its way. At the bottom of your soul, you know it's all over. Everything is draining away. This world is a cracked pipeline, a tanker run aground, vomiting the dregs of our lives all over the wretched landscape of a soiled universe. And your students know that, too. Just look in their eyes and see how deeply they know that this putrid world, this monstrous wreck, is their only inheritance. They know, but they don't realize. And you will help them realize. You will grant them the gift of realizing the truth of humanity. A true humanities education!"

His hand danced and shone, a knot of flames in the wailing light, and he brought it down like a comet of destruction to crash into the dull surface of the long table. Nothing impeded its fall. The book had disappeared, dissolved into nothingness.

And here's the basement. Watch your head, the ceiling's low down here. The key room's just this way. What? No, I don't need to get a key from the custodian. There's no key to the key room. Remember that. The key room is never locked, and anyone who dares can go right in. Keep that in mind, and you'll go far.

That was our first training, but it wasn't the last. As the consultant imparted his techniques to us, my colleagues and I began to acquire something of his quiet assurance. I'd spent my whole career thrashing in a sticky web of words—wrestling with difficult texts, weltering through student papers, grinding out lectures, articles, proposals—and every volume that evaporated at my touch was a loosening of the awful web, a blessed silence wrenched from cacophony. Most of the faculty felt the same. A new calm tempered the department's air of scurrying anxiety.

By the spring, we'd all learned the knack of making books vanish. Some of the more talented faculty had moved on from dissolving individual copies of books to obliterating the texts themselves, wiping whole novels and poems out of existence as if they'd never been written, and then on from literary texts to movies, songs, albums, TV shows. No false modesty here—I was the most talented of all. By winter break, I'd erased three Victorian triple-decker novels, two early Rolling Stones B-sides, and a beloved masterpiece of Finnish cinema called *The Reindeer Wept*. Never heard of it, have you? Exactly.

Not every member of the department was as gifted or as eager as I was, but only one of them truly resisted the consultant's program. Professor Tryon simply refused to abandon the notion that there was some inherent value in the humanities and that it was our task, our noble task, to inspire students with a love of literature and art, to teach them critical thinking, to make them life-long learners, and blah blah blah. You can imagine how hollow that nonsense sounded to me, who had felt a book turn to nothing under my hand, and who knew that a book could turn to nothing only because it had never been anything. Just a bit of filthy slime draining away, oozing through the cracks.

Even so, I hadn't fully accepted the consultant's teaching into my soul. What held me back was Professor Tryon herself. Our friendship. My love, held in my heart like a secret pearl. The way she made my daughter laugh. The way her breath felt on my cheek, soft and warm.

The crisis came at the end of the spring semester. The state legislature's cuts were even more drastic than we'd expected. The public education budget was slashed to the bone. Rumors swirled around campus that the administration was going to disband our department, get rid of the humanities altogether.

Professor Tryon was in a frenzy. She sent an email to the entire department, demanding an emergency meeting to discuss how we would resist the coming onslaught. When Professor Casimir demurred, she scheduled the meeting herself. It would take place on a Thursday evening in the seminar room where we usually met, and though it was not on the official department calendar, we all knew that everyone, even Professor Casimir, would attend.

And this is the key room. After you! No, don't bother with the light switch. The lights don't work in here. I'll just use the flashlight on my phone. Be sure to stay close to me; I know the way, but it's easy to get lost or stumble in the dark. Lots of things to trip over, lots of junk lying around. All sorts of trash and garbage. You might want to cover your nose.

But it's nice in here all the same, isn't it? No fluorescents. No infernal humming.

Professor Tryon's meeting was as wild and chaotic as you'd expect. She stood at the head of the long table, shouting and waving her arms, telling us we'd all be a bunch of cowards if we didn't stand up for ourselves.

"Stand up how?" someone shouted back. "What can we do?"

"What the fuck kind of question is that?" she screamed. "What you should be asking is, what can *they* do without *us*? They need us! This is a goddamn college, and we're the ones who do the goddamn teaching!"

I'd brought my daughter to the meeting, thinking it would be quick and we could catch the latest Pixar movie afterward. Blushing, I bent down to whisper in her ear. "Sorry about Professor Tryon's pottymouth, sweetie. She's just upset."

My daughter rolled her eyes. "I've heard way worse."

A sudden crash behind me brought me upright. Cold air gusted against my back, eddying through my hair like questing tendrils. I turned to see the consultant in the doorway, his glasses white with fluorescent splendor. His hand was extended in front of him, trembling, ecstatic. Everyone fell silent. The lights' hum was the shriek of a star devouring itself, collapsing into final darkness.

"What do you want?" Professor Tryon said at last.

The consultant smiled. "I want to help you." As he advanced, the assembled faculty parted before him, cringing away from his flickering hand.

"We've had enough of your help," Professor Tryon said. "We're not going to listen to any more of your bullshit. We're going to fight, and we're going to win."

The consultant approached the head of the table. I turned my daughter away from him, squeezed her against me.

"I'm not here to convince you," the consultant said. "If the department decides that my services are no longer required, I'll accept that decision. I'm not exactly hurting for work, you know. I'm not here because I need to be, or even because I want to be. I'm here because you need me. You need help, Professor Tryon. Let me help you."

"Go fuck yourself," Professor Tryon said. "Don't say one more word to me."

The consultant nodded. Without a word, he raised his transfigured hand to his face and removed his glasses.

I was standing behind the consultant, looking over his shoulder at Professor Tryon. I never saw his eyes without the glasses. But I saw what happened to Professor Tryon's face as she stared into those eyes. I saw the fight drain out of her. I saw her eyes' gleam of defiant hope gutter out. I saw her soul die.

The consultant raised his hand again, replaced his glasses. He held the spread palm out toward Professor Tryon, his fingers quivering inches from her face.

"No!" my daughter screamed. While I'd been watching Professor Tryon, she'd turned back toward the consultant, and now she struggled out of my grip and dashed toward him. "Don't you dare touch her!"

Before I could move, before I could open my mouth, the consultant whirled around, and the hand that had been reaching for Professor Tryon's face came down on my daughter's head.

When she dissolved, a quiet fell over the room, so deep I couldn't even hear the hum of the lights. The consultant's hand floated in empty air, motionless as the hand of a statue before it's cut from the marble. Motionless as a stone in the windless light of the world's ultimate sunset.

I looked into the consultant's eyes, calm and placid in their glass cage. I looked over his shoulder at Professor Tryon, her face totally empty, her eyes seeing nothing, seeing everything. I looked at the consultant's hand floating in the emptiness that had been my daughter.

I felt nothing. My heart was an empty tomb, cracked and drained. My education was complete.

I stretched out my hand. The consultant took it. We shook.

"I know things seem hopeless," the consultant said. "I know these cuts go deep, and they make it seem like there's no way for this department to continue its mission. But if you'll just think about what we've talked about over this past year, all the things we've helped each other learn and realize, I think you'll see that if we just knuckle down, and tighten our belts, and do more with less, and remember why we chose this career—it wasn't about the money, no, not about the money, it was about the love, wasn't it, yes, the love, the love, the love ..."

"Yes," I said. Tears spilled from my eyes. "Love."

It seems like we've been in this key room a long time, doesn't it? I'll bet you're asking yourself how far does this goddamn room go on, how far can we trudge along down here in the dark, threading our way between these heaps of junk, these piles of rotting garbage everywhere? How long can this fucking death march last?

Well, just hold your horses. We're getting close. See that gleam up ahead?

It didn't take long for me and the consultant to convince the rest of the faculty that our plan would work. It's pretty simple, when you think about it. When your resources are cut, you have to look at your expenses. What are the major expenses of a college? Well, administration's a big one. So, you dissolve the administration. But that's just the start. Facilities and services, that's another big one. And who demands those facilities and services? Students, of course. So, you dissolve the students. Next, there's non-administrative staff, counselors and custodians and so on. Dissolve them. And what's left? Faculty. That's a tricky one. After all, it's the faculty who were doing the dissolving. But you know what they say—how do you eat an elephant? One bite at a time.

Most of the faculty were no trouble. Even Professor Casimir ... *especially* Professor Casimir. To tell the truth, I think he was grateful to pass the reins over to me. He'd been department head a long time, and that sort of position will wear anyone down. I'm sure it won't be long before it wears me down, too.

A couple of the adjuncts got a bit feisty. Tried to organize a union, get a little collective action going. But we nipped that in the bud before it could cause any real problems.

Oh, I almost forgot one big expense, something colleges spend a lot of money on. Can you guess? That's right—consultants! But I suppose it's the sign of a good consultant that their clients eventually outgrow the need for them. They're like teachers in that way. No prouder moment for a teacher than when your student outpaces you.

In the end, it was just me and Professor Tryon. I hoped it could stay that way, that the two of us could keep working together forever, doing what we love. But it wasn't meant to be. Maybe the consultant's eyes looked too deep into her, hollowed her out too completely. If there's nothing left, nothing at all, then nothing can drain out. And that's what life is, wouldn't you say? A gradual process of draining out? Draining away, drop by drop?

What are you giving me that look for? Is it something I said?

Oh, I see. You really are an aficionado of the humanities, a true close reader. A little while ago, when I said my heart was an empty tomb, all drained out, you made a note of it. Maybe you thought it was a nice little image, or maybe you thought it was a silly, melodramatic cliché. Anyhow, you filed it away. And then when I said that Professor Tryon was totally drained and hollow, so that she couldn't keep going ... implying that, since

I'm still here talking to you, I'm *not* totally drained ... well, isn't that a bit of a contradiction?

Unless, you're thinking with your clever little analyzing brain, unless I've been *replenished* from time to time ... unless I keep filling up that cracked, broken heart of mine, filling it up so that it drains out again, then filling it again, and again ...

And now you understand. I see in your eyes that you understand. But now something else is bothering you. If I'm leading you to your doom, leading you through this darkness and filth to a fate that's surely worse than anything you can imagine, why are you still here? Why aren't you running away, screaming for help? Wouldn't any fate—lost in the dark forever, crushed in a landslide of garbage, eaten by rats and cockroaches—wouldn't any terrible end be better than what awaits you, if you come with me?

Yes, it would.

So, why aren't you running away?

Let me ask about something you may not have noticed, even with your feisty adjunct mind. When was the last time I spoke out loud? Think about it. I believe you'll find it was when we were upstairs, standing at your office door. I said something like, "Try jiggling the knob." Since then, you've been hearing my voice, but I haven't been speaking. I've been in your mind, pulling you along on a leash of words. Draining you out, bit by bit.

The consultant's hand was a fearsome weapon, dazzling and swift, but crude. Swish, pop, disappear. My own hand has developed much subtler techniques. If you think back again to our conversation upstairs, you may recall I gave you a reassuring pat on the shoulder.

We're almost there. See! The lights that glare like bursting stars reflected in the eyes of a dead world! Listen! The hum that raves like a billion flies at feast!

Oh, stop blubbering. What are you losing, really? You're a humanities adjunct, you probably would have frozen to death in your car over winter break.

Here we are. Just look into the light. Just let the hum wash over you. Soon you'll remember why you chose this career, and you'll find it's not so hard to do more with less.

Estrangements

Garrett stepped into the living room, saw his children sitting cross-legged on the rug in front of the television, and screamed. Jessica and Tim's faces were gone, their skulls wrapped in a vile substance like greasy, pinkish-gray leather. Holes pocked the moist surface of the covering—purulent holes where dark flecks floated in pale jelly, narrow holes that flexed and shuddered obscenely, gaping holes housing coarse red worms that squirmed and writhed over shards of upthrust bone. Staring at the things that had been his children, now hideous, faceless freaks, Garrett howled in shock and terror.

"Oh my God, honey, what is it? What's wrong?"

Garrett spun toward his husband's voice. Terry stood in the doorway of the kitchen, an oven mitt on one hand and a spatula in the other. Concern and confusion shone from his wide, startled eyes.

"The kids, they're ..." Turning back toward the children, Garrett felt his throat and chest clench, choking his words. He pressed a hand to his sternum and breathed slowly, in and out, until the knot around his heart loosened.

Jessica and Tim looked up at him, open-mouthed. They were the same beautiful children he'd tucked into bed last night, with the same adorable faces, now slack with surprise. Tim's lip quivered.

"What's wrong, Daddy?" Jessica said. Always the brave one, she kept her voice calm and steady, but her left thumb tapped nervously against the cast that bound her right forearm.

"I thought I saw …" Garrett shivered at the thought of those terrible not-faces. Banishing the image with a shake of his head, he smiled sheepishly. "Sorry if I scared you, kids. My eyes were playing tricks on me. Must still be half-asleep."

"Then you'd better come in here and get yourself some coffee," Terry said, beckoning with his mitted hand as he receded into the kitchen. Garrett thought he saw an anxious glint in his husband's eyes, but maybe it was a gleam of amused relief, or just another figment of his own imagination. He decided not to worry about it.

Leaning next to the sink, Garrett sipped his coffee and watched Terry arrange cinnamon toast, scrambled eggs and bacon on the row of plates beside the stove. Now that his momentary fright—waking dream? hallucination?—had passed, Garrett savored the elements of the family's Saturday morning ritual. The kids in the living room watching videos, Terry in the kitchen preparing breakfast, himself taking it easy and making a list of the chores he'd tackle in the afternoon. Go to the farmer's market, mow the lawn, take out the trash. Everything in its place, as deliciously familiar as the 15-year-old indie rock songs drifting from Terry's phone on the counter.

The buzz of a text interrupted the music. Terry glanced at his phone, frowned.

"Bad news?" Garrett said.

"Not sure." Terry slid the last strips of bacon onto a plate. "It's my sister. Vague as usual. She just says, *Are you seeing this?*"

Garrett chuckled. Typical Laura. "Well, are you?"

"Beats me." Terry cleared his throat. "Hey, do you think you'll have time to trim those dead branches today?"

Garrett sighed, hearing the part Terry was too nice to say: If you'd done it a week ago, Jessica wouldn't have broken her arm falling out of the tree. Sawing the cankered limbs from the maple in the yard had been on his to-do list for months, but he'd kept putting it off, and now he was paying the price in dubious looks, veiled insinuations. "I'll do it right after breakfast," he said.

"Thanks, honey." Terry leaned in, gave him a peck on the cheek. "Grab the kids' plates, will you?"

"Sure thing. Just one more sip." He swigged the last of his coffee. Terry left the kitchen, a plate in each hand.

The clang of shattering ceramic brought Garrett to the doorway. Terry stood frozen in the living room, halfway to the breakfast table, chunks of porcelain mixed with heaps of food at his feet. His empty hands hovered waist-high in front of him as he trembled, choked whimpers struggling from his throat. On the other side of the room, Jessica and Tim stood staring at their second terrified parent of the morning.

Garrett hurried over, careful to keep his bare feet clear of the fragments of plate. Thinking of his own weird vision, he assumed Terry would be looking at the children, perhaps seeing those same revolting, hole-ridden swaths, but instead Terry was gazing at his own hands, his eyes full of fear and incredulity.

"What the fuck are those things?" Terry whispered. His fingers flexed and quivered. "What are they doing?"

Garrett put what he hoped was a reassuring hand on Terry's shoulder. "What things? You mean your hands?"

"Those aren't my hands. Those are ... they're ..."

"Baby, look at me." Garrett rubbed his thumb gently against Terry's neck. "Just look at me for a second."

It seemed to take a tremendous effort for Terry to pull his gaze away from his hands. His whole body quaked and strained. When he finally raised his eyes to meet Garrett's, his pupils were so dilated it was like staring into two black pits. Garrett thought he saw something move at the bottom of those pits, something that twitched and glimmered, and for a moment he wondered if he might be seeing Terry's brain, its pale whorls cringing in horror.

Terry blinked. His pupils contracted. His glance flicked back to his hands, and Garrett saw the tension drain out of him as he heaved a tremendous sigh. "What the hell is going on?" he murmured.

Wrapping an arm around Terry's shoulders, Garrett steered him to the breakfast table, swerving to avoid the shards and scraps that littered the floor. Tim and Jessica had vanished from the living room—retreated to their bedroom, Garrett supposed, to wait for their parents to start acting normal again.

Terry slid into a chair and slumped forward, shaking his head. Garrett placed a hand lightly in the middle of his husband's back.

"What did you see?" Garrett said.

"Monsters," Terry said. "Two monsters floating in front of me. Pale and slimy-looking, with thick, veiny bodies and little hairs sprouting out. They had five heads apiece, with long, jointed necks. Each head had one big pink eye, and all of the eyes were staring up at me."

"Anything else you remember?"

"One of the necks had a metal collar around it, the kind you might hitch a chain to. Like the thing had escaped from a dungeon."

Garrett slid his palm up Terry's back, along his shoulder, down his left arm. Lifting Terry's hand, he held it out over the table and ran his thumb along the fingers, over the pink fingernails. He tapped his thumbnail on the wedding band that gleamed on Terry's finger like a silver collar.

"Oh my fucking God," Terry said, a shudder of revulsion shaking his voice. "I could have sworn ..."

"It's okay," Garrett said. "Just a trick of your eyes. One of those weird things."

Terry twisted in the chair, looked into Garrett's face. "What about you, honey? What did you see?"

Closing his eyes, Garrett saw them again—the greasy not-faces, the disgusting holes, the things glinting and squirming in the hollows. Something in the memory shifted, some subtle change of light, and suddenly he realized what he'd been looking at, what had made him scream with terror. Skin, eyes, noses, mouths, tongues ...

"The kids," he said. "I saw the kids, but it didn't look like them. It looked like ..."

"Monsters," Terry said.

They stared at one another, saying nothing. In the quiet, Garrett heard music drifting faintly from the kitchen, Terry's phone still playing the jagged guitars and swooping synths of their youth. The music faded for a moment, the hush of an incoming text. It faded again, again.

Terry rose, crossed the living room. As he passed through the doorway into the kitchen, Garrett glimpsed a shambling, misshapen creature, stiff tubes and knobs of flesh trailing from a central bulk wrapped in gauzy cloth as if bandaged to hide the scars of some mutilation. The grotesque beast slid into the mouth of a larger creature, disappeared down its gullet.

That's Terry, Garrett thought. *He's going into the kitchen.* But it didn't look like Terry.

The music fell silent. Garrett's breath rasped in his throat, his pulse hammered in his ears. His husband, their children, their house, their own bodies, the most familiar things in the world

... was it some delusion, making them look monstrous? Or was it the familiarity itself falling away, revealing what was always underneath, unseen?

What the fuck was happening?

When Terry emerged from the kitchen, he looked like Terry again, but his expression filled Garrett with dread. He approached the breakfast table, his phone clutched in his hand. "More messages from Laura," he said.

Garrett took the phone, open to the message app. Collapsing into a chair, he read the texts from Terry's sister.

Are you seeing this?

Seriously bro this is crazy. Did you see the news?

The next message was a link to a news story. The preview image showed a woman with blood running down the side of her face, a car overturned in the street behind her. Below the image, the headline read, *BREAKING: Deadly incidents around the world, trance-like states and acts of violence reported.*

Laura's messages continued. *Text me back Terry, or call or email, whatever. Something is seriously fucked up, we're getting scared. Love u*

If you see this don't bother texting back just go to the nearest hospital, they think it's probably some kind of medical thing infection or whatever and when they figure out a treatment hospital's where they'll have it so just go. Go now as soon as you see this go

ddnjfkdsbfgiabhsdif

FUCK GO NOW sdjnbkjdfs

gggggggg

The chunk of charred bone flashed in Garrett's hand. He hurled the thing away with a yelp, and it clattered over the scales of the monstrous maw where he sat, coming to rest at the edge of a flat, scabbed tongue.

Terry's feet whispered on the floorboards. He picked up his phone where it lay next to the rug, the rug where Tim and Jessica had sat cross-legged in front of the television, watching videos. He gazed at Garrett, his eyes wary.

"We should get the kids out of here," Garrett said. "Go to the hospital, like Laura said. Get out of the house, at least. Maybe there's some kind of gas or toxin in here, some kind of leak, you know? Something that causes hallucinations?"

Terry frowned at his phone. "This news story she sent says it's happening all over the world. People not recognizing things, mistaking other people for ... creatures. Attacking them."

"Attacking?" Garrett recalled what he thought he'd seen. Those wretched, faceless things, abominations that shouldn't live. If his vision hadn't gone back to normal, what would he have done? Would the horror of the sight have driven him to violence, repugnance forcing him to assault his own children?

No. I love them too much to ever hurt them. Some part of my mind would have known, would have stopped me.

The shambling bulk—*Terry*—Terry held out the phone toward Garrett. It showed the story from the link Laura had sent. A video was playing, a woman speaking. "I thought it was an animal," she said. Tears and blood streaked her face. "Some kind of deformed, vicious animal. It was coming at me, and

I panicked. I grabbed the closest thing I could get my hands on, and I started hitting it. I just wanted it to go away, but it wouldn't go away, it kept coming, it was roaring and screaming at me, so I just kept hitting. And then it fell down, and I ... I hit it some more and then ... and then I saw ..." The woman closed her eyes, covered her mouth with her hands. As she began to scream, the video ended.

Terry lowered the phone to his side. "'Acute agnosia,' they're calling it," he said. "No one knows why it's happening."

Garrett grimaced. "So we should all go to the hospital, to be there when they figure it out."

"I say we stay here," Terry said. "The hospital's going to be crowded. The more people, the more danger. Do you really want to put the kids in that kind of situation?"

"I'll keep the kids safe."

"Like you kept Jessica safe?"

A stab of anger and guilt stung Garrett's heart, made him gasp. "Why would you say that? Do you think I ...?"

Terry shook his head. "I'm sorry. I didn't mean that. But what if it comes back, this thing, this disease or whatever? You've already had a flash of it. How will you keep the kids safe if you don't know who they are?"

Garrett swallowed his shame and frustration, his pointless urge to defend himself. "I'll know. I'm sure of it. We'll go to the hospital, and then we'll—"

The words caught in his throat as Terry's eyes filled with darkness, pupils opening like midnight flowers. Terry's lips peeled back from his teeth, his hands rising, twisting into claws.

"Hey!" Garrett rushed to his husband, wrapped his arms around him and held him close. "Hey, baby, it's me. It's Garrett. It's going to be okay."

A rancid mass of flesh squirmed in his arms, snarling and squealing. A sticky membrane pressed against his cheek. He closed his eyes tight. *Terry, Terry, Terry …*

Terry relaxed against him, sobbing, his head on his shoulder. "Oh my God, oh my God."

Garrett rubbed his hands along Terry's back, murmured in his ear. "You see? It's okay. We'll get through this." Still holding Terry tight, he maneuvered him to the breakfast table and down into a chair. "Now just sit here for a minute while I get the kids. We're going to the hospital."

The door to the kids' bedroom stood ajar. Garrett tapped a knuckle against the door, pushing it slowly open. The room was dark. "Jessica? Tim?" He flicked on the lights.

At first he thought the bedroom was empty. He swept his eyes across the unmade beds, the clothes and toys scattered around, wondering where the kids had gone. Then he saw them, huddled on the floor between the beds. Two lumps of misbegotten foulness, throbbing meat wrapped in slimy casings. Unnatural, unworthy of existence.

Your children. Your children.

"Daddy," one of the things—*Tim*—said. "Daddy, I'm scared."

Garrett took a deep breath, struggling to master his own terror. "I know, sweetie. We're all scared. But we need to go to the hospital."

The other thing—*Jessica*—widened its dark-flecked, pus-filled holes—*eyes*, her eyes. The cast on her arm gleamed like exposed bone. "Are you sick, Daddy? Is Papa sick? Is that why you've been shouting?"

"A lot of people are getting sick, and we need to go to the hospital so we'll be first in line to get the medicine."

As the things rose and approached him, Garrett saw them flickering back and forth, now his beloved children, now grotesque horrors. *Like that picture that's a duck one moment, a rabbit the next, depending on how you look at it.* He tried to force himself to see them as children, but he could feel his mind slipping, losing its grasp on their childness, their familiar humanity. He gritted his teeth with the effort of seeing them as they were, as he knew them, loved them. "Hurry," he said.

Terry was still sitting at the breakfast table, his arms rigid at his sides. "Come on, baby," Garrett called from the entryway. "We're going." Terry closed his eyes, pressed his hands over his ears.

Behind Garrett, one of the things made a chittering, hissing sound. He turned. "What did you say, sweetie?"

"I said, Papa's sick, isn't he?" Jessica whispered, her tongue's red worm writhing.

"Yes, he's sick. So the three of us will go to the hospital first, and once we've got the medicine, we'll come back for Papa."

Garrett snatched the keys from the table in the entryway, led the kids outside. The maple swayed its dead limbs above the sparkling lawn as a siren keened in the distance. Down the block, a house was burning, smoke staining the sky. Garrett herded the kids into the car, and for a moment, the five-year-old Honda was a chitinous beast, devoured faces staring out in terror from its transparent belly, but Garrett wrestled his mind into seeing it as a car. He got in, turned the key in the ignition, began to back out into the street.

Tim leaned forward in the passenger seat. "Papa!" he cried.

At the sound of his voice, Garrett braked instinctively and looked toward the house. The misshapen creature shambled from the front door to the driveway, flailing its tubes and swinging its bulbous knob from side to side. Even as Garrett screamed, he tried to recognize the thing, to remember the name he used to call it, but sheer, stark fear—fear for himself, fear for the children—overwhelmed him, loosened his mind's grip. The monster howled and squealed, waving jointed appendages that branched into gruesome, claw-tipped tentacles. A thing that should not, must not exist. Garrett put the car into drive.

The impact knocked the creature against the garage door. It slumped down, smearing dark ichor across the white surface. Garrett quickly reversed and surged forward again, crushing the thing against the sullied door. There was a squelch, a crack, a moan. When Garrett backed up, the tires crunched over the monster's vile limbs.

The children were screaming so loud, Garrett could hardly remember where they needed to go. *The hospital, the hospital.* He wrenched the car around, sped toward the edge of town, the medical center, just as he'd done a week earlier as his daughter whimpered and writhed in the backseat. The moment she'd fallen, he'd leapt into action, brought her to safety. He'd do it again.

"Papa, Papa!" Jessica shrieked behind him.

"I told you, we'll come back for Papa once we've got the medicine," Garrett said.

"Why did you do that, Daddy?" Tim wailed.

"I had to ... that thing ... that, that monster ..." A cloud was gathering over Garrett's mind. He had a good reason for what he'd done, he was sure of it, but he couldn't quite remember what the reason was. The car flashed past figures staggering on the sidewalk, figures crawling in the road, clawing at each other. The children were screaming so loud ... he couldn't think ... so loud ...

Something hit him on the shoulder. It hit him again, harder. When he turned his head to see what it was, it hit him in the face.

"What are you?" Jessica screamed, her eyes shining with horror. "What did you do with my daddy?" She raised her arm, and Garrett saw the skeletal gleam of the cast a moment before it struck him in the eye.

Light exploded across his vision. He whipped his head around to escape the next blow, but the movement sent his hands sliding left along the steering wheel, and the car went into a sharp turn. He'd been going too fast, rushing to get to the hospital, to get away from that thing whose name he couldn't remember, didn't want to remember. Still half-blind, he slammed on the brakes. The car skidded, spun off the road, rolled. Garrett felt his mind fly apart.

When he opened his eyes, he didn't know how much time had passed, couldn't remember where he was, where he'd come from or where he'd been going. Nothing felt familiar. He was sitting sideways, his face resting against a cold, flat surface. In front of him was another surface, cracked and shattered. He was in an enclosure, some type of cage or dungeon, and two shapeless creatures had been shut in with him. The creatures weren't moving. *Asleep*, he thought. He hoped so.

After a while, he managed to crawl forward through the broken surface and out of the cage. His body hurt, and he could tell that some parts of him were damaged, but he didn't know which parts, what they were called. He could stand, at least. He looked around. Shapes, colors. Nothing he recognized. He vaguely remembered he'd been going somewhere. He walked in what he thought was the right direction.

As he walked, the things around him changed. Unfamiliar things gave way to other, equally unfamiliar things. The only thing that stayed the same was the expanse overhead, the blue field with the white fleck floating across it. There was a name for that, he remembered, a fleck in a bright field. *Eye?* Yes.

He walked on, keeping his gaze fixed on the eye overhead, even though its unblinking stare hurt to look at. It was worth a little pain, after all, to have something that stayed the same while everything else changed. When the pain grew too fierce, the stare too piercing, he closed his own eyes and walked in darkness.

Exuviae

My big sisters look exactly alike. Two of them stand by my bedside, their mouthparts moving in flawless synchrony. "Grandmother wants to see you," they say.

The long sleep has numbed my limbs. I stumble down the upstairs hallway, a sister supporting me on either side. Half-open doors slide past, offering glimpses of the shadowy nurseries where my nieces lie swaddled in their uncles.

At the end of the hallway, my sisters shove me into Grandmother's room and shut the door behind me. The cavernous space is lit only by a floor lamp with a green shawl draped over its shade. Grandmother stands in the far corner, her eyes glistening in the dimness, the air thick with her cold, heavy breath.

Grandmother's joints creak and pop as she approaches me. Her stinger drags along the floor. My legs tremble, and I lean against the wall for support. Its pulpy surface moistens my hands.

Grandmother's eyes are the biggest I've ever seen. She looks me up and down. "You're close to term, child," she says, her voice a buzzing rasp.

"A few days, my sisters say."

"That means an empty bed. Who'll fill that bed, I wonder?"

I know what's expected of me. I lift my chin and swallow the fear coiled in my throat. "I'll find you a new granddaughter, ma'am."

She raises a thin foreleg, runs a claw gently down my cheek. In the green dimness, her gaze shimmers almost like love.

Downstairs, the living room is full of family. Big sisters crowd around the table, a swarm of aunts on the ceiling, a rotting heap of half-eaten uncles in the corner. Another little sister, the newest, stands trembling against the wall, her arms wrapped nervously around her stomach. She must have wandered from her bedroom. The light of the bare, dangling bulb gleams on her shaved head, on the black wells of her eyes.

Pity floods me, drowning the thought of my errand. The girl seems so lost, so ill at ease in her new home. In the first days after my induction, I must have looked the same way.

I sidle up next to her and force what I hope is a comforting smile. "How are you feeling, little sister?"

"I feel okay, little sister. Thank you." Her voice is shaky and quiet, almost a whisper. Her gaze is fixed on the table and the spindly forms gathered there.

"Don't worry," I say. "They're not paying attention to us."

"How do you know? What are they doing?"

"They're praying."

The girl's senses haven't sharpened enough to hear those high, chirping voices that scrape at my ears like crushed glass. Somewhere beneath perception, though, their prayer reaches her. She shudders, turns her head away. At the top of her neck, the induction mark glistens, red and swollen.

I raise a hand to my own nape. My hair's grown long again, but the mark is easy to find, a rough, puckered mouth among the curls.

Feeling the scar brings my errand back to mind, along with a fresh stab of compassion for the girl. How terrified she must be, how lonely, how confused. When I was new to the house, I would have given anything for a kind word, a human glance.

"Little sister," I say. She turns back toward me, tears shining on her cheeks. "I'm going out. Do you want to come with me?"

She darts an anxious glance toward the chittering, jointed things around the table. "Will they ..."

"It's fine. They know I'm running an errand."

When she realizes what that means, her mouth falls open and her eyes widen, but she quickly masters her revulsion. She gives me a small, determined smile, a smile that says she'd do anything at all rather than have me leave her in this house with our big sisters, our aunts and uncles, Grandmother.

I take her trembling hand. "Let's go."

The moment I open the front door, the room behind us fills with screeching. The girl yanks her hand from mine, whirls around with a terrified gasp. I turn and touch her shoulder, hoping to calm her.

Above our big sisters' bowed, angular heads, our aunts howl on the ceiling, fluttering their hindwings and flailing their antennae. Their eyes glare and swivel, almost as big as Grandmother's.

"It's okay," I whisper into the girl's ear. "They're not angry at us. They're just hungry."

A dirt road runs between fields of coarse grass that were green and sweet-smelling when I was brought to the house, slumped in the passenger seat of a rusted-out station wagon while a little sister drove. Now I drive that same car through a gray, withered expanse under a gray sky, the girl sitting ramrod-straight beside me with her hands folded in her lap.

Did I know how to drive before I came to the house, or did I learn while I slept, my niece whispering instructions in my ear from the inside? I can't remember.

After so long in the house, the world horrifies me with its breadth and brightness. Every jolt of the wheels on the pitted dirt sends a wave of panic through me, as if the station wagon is about to fly off into an infinite distance. Soon, I'm longing for the house's closed-in world, its endless, whispering twilight behind plywood-covered windows. I want to talk to the girl, if only to distract myself from the vastness all around, but my head is full of chirping, buzzing, screeching, a swarm of noise choking all human words.

When the girl finally speaks, her voice stills the clatter in my brain. "What's your name?" she says.

"It's …" A shadowy syllable wavers at the bottom of my mind, but it fades before my tongue can grasp it. "It's little sister. I had another one, but I lost it in my sleep."

"You sleep a lot. You've been sleeping since they brought me."

"Sleep ripens the sisterhood. It takes a long time. I woke up every day or two at first, but after a while I stayed asleep."

"I don't like sleeping in that house." Her voice quavers, panic-tinged, but when I glance away from the road her face is calm. "My dreams make me forget things."

"That's the ripening." I tap a finger against the back of my neck, the hidden scar. "The niece goes in and makes you a sister. While you sleep, she's eating up the old parts of you, making you new. You have to forget the old way before you can learn the new way."

"I don't want to forget. I want to stay me. My name is Clara. I want to keep it."

My heart breaks for her. Before the long sleep, I felt the same way, seeing only the terrible side of the transformation. Now, I've begun to feel the wonder, the miracle of it. "It's not so bad to change," I say. "When the old parts of you go away, the fear goes away, too. I used to be as scared as you are, Clara. I'm still scared now, but only a little. Mostly, I'm happy, because I'm part of a real family where everyone belongs and we all have a place." As I say it, I find myself believing it more and more. I smile. "In a few more days, I won't be scared at all. I'll be completely ripe. I'll be a big sister."

———◆———

We sit in the lee of the little house, watching columns of dust swirl as the wind sweeps across the neighboring field. The road that runs in front of the house is completely empty. The station wagon parked on the roadside is a rust-colored speck in the distance. Nothing else in sight but dust and wind and dead grass and darkening sky.

My little sister's been silent since we arrived. Is she frozen with terror, lost in thought, waiting for something? I can't tell. She can't be listening to the sounds from inside the house, the father and daughter talking as they move from room to room. Her ears aren't keen enough yet.

At last, she breaks her silence. "Is this how they got you?" she whispers.

"Yes," I whisper back. The memories surge up out of swirling darkness—waking up in my old bed, my old room, the stars through the open window. The little sister's head silhouetted against the stars. The little sister's hand covering my mouth, the poison of her changed skin overwhelming me.

Waking up again in the station wagon. Being dragged across the yard into the house. That awful first glimpse of the big sisters' jointed limbs and bulging eyes. The aunts' famished hissing. The uncle's lips pressed against my neck as the niece that had hatched in his guts squirmed out of his mouth, her tiny teeth rasping my flesh. The aunts' shrieks of delight as they feasted on the spent, moaning uncle, tearing gobbets out of him with their mandibles.

I squeeze my eyes shut and wait for the memories to subside. Those things happened to someone else, I tell myself, someone whose name you can't even remember. Just think of what you've gained at the price of a little fear, a little pain. Think of your wonderful new family.

Are those really my thoughts, or is it just my niece whispering lies as she chews up the last bits of me?

It doesn't matter. The family is what matters. My niece in my head is me. The big sister I'll be in a few days is me. When the big sister's shiny carapace cracks, the aunt that squirms out will be me, and the egg the aunt lays in an uncle's flesh will be me. When the aunt's work is done and Grandmother bites her head off, it will be my own jaws rending my own body, my own stinger quivering in my own guts.

The sun has set behind the clouds. The lights in the little house have gone out. "It's time," I murmur. "Do you want to come get her with me?"

My little sister trembles with cold, or fear, or memory. "No," she whispers.

I rise in the darkness and creep along the side of the house to the daughter's bedroom window. Through the glass, I can hear her steady breathing. The window slides open as quietly as I'd hoped, and I make no noise as I slip through.

The room is pitch-dark, but with my sharpened eyes I see the daughter lying on her side, her legs tucked against her chest and the blanket tight around her chin. As I approach the bed, she stirs in her sleep, the blanket rippling like an uncle's belly with a wriggling niece inside, but she doesn't wake.

Gently, lovingly, I reach for my new sister.

A storm of noise shatters the silence. Fists pounding on the door of the little house, a ragged voice shrieking from outside. Clara's voice. "Wake up! Wake up! She's coming to get you!"

The daughter's eyes snap open. Her scream mingles with Clara's keening howls. I clamp my fingers over her mouth, but there's no time to put her to sleep that way. I need a faster, stronger poison. My fingers worm between her lips, and once I've pried her jaws open, I lean down and spit into her mouth. She gags and splutters, but my changed juices are already working on her, numbing her tissues. After a moment, she's sleeping more soundly than ever.

A crash thunders behind me as the bedroom door slams against the wall. I whirl to see the father rush into the room, a metal bat clutched in his hand. "Get away from her!" he shouts, running at me. Behind him, I glimpse another dark room, another open door, the empty night beyond. Clara stands on the threshold, her face slack, paralyzed with horror.

I leap toward the open window, but the father swings furiously and the bat clangs against my skull. Something in my head cracks, and I fall to the floor with a wail of shock and pain. The father swings the bat again, hits me in the hip. Another crack. With a writhing lunge, I get my fingers around his ankles. He totters but doesn't fall. I'm still wailing, my voice rising and rising, higher than any human can hear.

Another lunge forward, and I sink my teeth through the thin fabric of his pajamas and into his calf. He roars with pain and swings again, again. My arm splinters, not the bone but the arm, the hard shell that's grown inside the skin. I feel my niece squirming inside my broken head, straining to bring me to ripeness before my life drains out. The father's blood is hot in my mouth. I shove my tongue into the wound I've opened, slathering the bite with venom.

The metal bat rings against the floor. The father crumples and falls.

I'm too shattered to stand. With my unbroken arm, I drag myself across the father's convulsing body toward the window. Stretching up as far as I can, I curl my fingers on the edge of the sill, but I'm too weak to lift myself. I slump against the wall, my head lolling.

Feet shuffle outside the room. I lift my eyes. Clara trembles in the doorway, her cheeks slimy with tears.

I do my best to smile. "It's all right," I mumble. "I forgive you, little sister."

A tide of sleep rises around me, darker than the darkness. The last thing I hear before oblivion swallows me is my little sister's footsteps running through the house, out into the night.

Something hard and sharp presses against my temple. Hard yet gentle, sharp yet delicate. As it moves across my face, my skin sloughs off, but there's no pain. I feel unbound, as if I've spent my whole life wrapped in damp paper. I'm emerging from myself.

When the sharp thing moves over my eyes, cutting the lids away, I can see again. A big sister's face looms close to mine, her eyes twitching with concern. I'm still slumped against the wall of the daughter's bedroom. Across the room, another big sister watches as the first's sharp-clawed forelegs strip off my husk.

My new face comes free of its soft, wet prison. I stretch my mouth, roll the great globes of my eyes. Even at the very end, I'd feared this ripening, this final departure from human flesh. Now that I've changed, I know there was never anything to fear. There is no final departure, only a chain of transformations leading onward through form after form.

"How did you find me, sisters?" I say. My new voice comes easily, its chirps and trills flowing sweetly from my mouthparts.

"You called out for us," the two of them say in unison. "We do not abandon our own."

I try to stand, but my legs only twitch. I look down at my new body and see a battered, twisted thing, my limbs cracked and thrown out of joint by the father's brutal assault.

"Lie still," my sisters say. "Let us help you."

They lift me carefully in their strong, hard arms. As we leave the bedroom, I see that a sheet of plywood covers the window, nailed to the wall with crude spikes.

My sisters carry me out into the front room of the little house. Here, too, the windows have been covered, and all the lamps are burning. Against one wall, the man who attacked me lies naked and unconscious on a leather couch. The leg I bit has been cut off at mid-thigh, the wound sealed with brownish-gray pulp. Blood trickles from a fresh incision just below his navel.

On the ceiling above the couch, an aunt clutches the man's severed leg in her foreclaws. Scraps of flesh drop from her nibbling jaws. The sound she's making is pure pleasure, almost a purr. Her ovipositor trembles behind her, its spear-tip red from the new uncle's guts.

"You did well," my sisters said. The pride in their voices fills me with joy.

"And the daughter?" I say.

They carry me to the open door of another room. Inside, the daughter lies on a wide, high bed with her legs curled against her chest, just as I first saw her. Next to her, on her back with her arms straight at her sides, lies Clara.

"Little sister!" I say, my voice shrill with relief. "Where did you find her?"

"She didn't get far," the big sisters say with satisfaction. "We do not abandon our own."

Something occurs to me, a sour note amid my happiness. I click my mouth in confusion. "But why are we still in this house, and not at Grandmother's?"

In the pause before they answer, I feel their compassion like a vibration in the air. "Because you cannot go there, sister. Your injuries are too great. You must remain here."

At first, I simply don't grasp what they're saying. The words seem as broken as my body, their meaning draining out like blood. When I finally understand, I feel a door slam shut in my mind. My house, my family, my life, all torn away. An endless, unbearable amputation. I twitch and flail, twisting feebly in my sisters' arms. A shriek wrenches itself from my chattering mouthparts.

"Hush, hush," they croon. "Be still, be still." They carry me to the daughter's bedroom, lay me down in the tangled sheets.

I'm ashamed of my outburst. That's not how a big sister should behave. I force myself to lie quiet. "I don't want to stay here by myself," I whisper.

"Must we say it again?" my sisters say. "We do not abandon our own."

"But ..."

"Listen. The family has conferred, decided what must be done. Surely you can guess the decision?"

I shake my head.

"Recall what you've seen already," my sisters say. "The family has sent an aunt to this house, and she's set a niece to hatch inside the uncle you found. Once the niece is ready, we have a vessel to put her in. We have a little sister sleeping the long sleep. And a pair of big sisters, too."

"And me," I say, still resisting the ultimate, incredible conclusion.

"And you. Just think of all you've done! You've fought boldly, suffered bravely for the sake of the family. And you've found this house. Not as big as the other house, true, but just as fine a hiding place. Who'll ever stop along that road? Who'll ever find us here? It's a perfect nest."

"But a nest needs ..."

Their eyes tremble with excitement. "Exactly."

We sit quietly together for a while, saying prayers to the infinite nest that embraces us all. Afterward, I sleep to regain my strength. When I wake, a bowl made of pulp sits by my bedside. The thick, pale jelly in the bowl tastes bitter, but I drink it eagerly. The jelly makes me sleepy. I wake again to find another bowl. I drink again, sleep again, wake, drink, sleep. My legs become longer, my eyes larger, my stinger thick and sharp. My breath grows cold and heavy, filling the room, moistening the walls. My heart swells to bursting with love and hunger.

I know I'll make a wonderful Grandmother.

Bite-Apple

Oh yes, I'll be sure to give her the pills every morning. Thank you for coming all this way, Doctor, and on Halloween, too.

I'm sure you're eager to get home and take your children trick-or-treating, but could you spare a minute to join us in a game before you leave? It won't take long, and it would make Sarah so happy. We don't get trick-or-treaters out here, and I can't take her to town, not with her condition. A holiday game would make it feel like a real Halloween.

Thank you so much, Doctor. You're so kind, so generous.

The game is simple. All we need is an apple, a string, and a hook. I bought a beautiful red apple at the market this morning, and there's a hook in the ceiling where Sarah used to hang her little fern. I'll cut a string from my old apron, and we'll have everything.

My grandmother taught me this game when I was Sarah's age. Grandma grew up very poor, and this is the kind of game even the poorest can play. Nothing fancy, just an apple you can pluck from any tree, a string you can dig from any trash-heap, and a hook—well, in the hovel Grandma grew up in, there must have been hooks sticking out all over.

How that old woman loved Halloween! The one night of the year, she used to say, when all the poor children go to the big houses and demand their due. A shadow of the reckoning where the last shall be first. A pious woman, my grandmother, in her way.

There, I've tied the string tight around the stem of the apple. Here's the other end of the string; would you mind looping it around the hook? It's a bit too high for me. I'm lucky to have such a tall playfellow!

Before I fetch Sarah, let's have a quick practice round. I'll set the apple swinging, and we'll take turns trying to hold it. The rule is, you can't use your hands, only your mouth. Bite the apple and hold it. Ready?

Oh, Doctor, didn't I just say you can't use your hands? How did you ever get that fancy degree if you can't follow a simple rule? I'm only teasing, of course. I know how hard it is, when that apple comes swinging right at you, not to reach up and grab it. Goodness knows how many times I grabbed the apple when I was a girl. Grandma used to smack me right across the face. "No hands, child!" she'd shout.

I won't smack you, Doctor, but if you'll allow me, I'll cut off the other string from my apron and tie your wrists. Not a tight knot, nothing you can't get out of. Just to remind you of the rule.

There, how's that? Good. Let's try again.

Why, Doctor, you're a natural! Such healthy teeth. I'll bet when you were a boy, you went to the best dentist in town. Not like me. When I had a toothache, my father would take me into the garage and yank the tooth out with a pair of pliers. I'd wake up the next morning with blood all over my pillow.

I know you're anxious to get back to your big house and your children. Two girls and two boys, isn't that right? Such a lucky man. So blessed.

Wait one moment. I'll fetch Sarah.

Sarah, honey, don't be frightened. This is the doctor, the one who took your temperature and felt your pulse. He's going to play a Halloween game with us. Isn't that nice? Aren't you grateful? No, don't speak. I know it hurts to speak. Just smile. He'll know what you mean.

I'm sure your children look wonderful in their expensive costumes, Doctor, but can any of them match my Sarah? Look at her thin arms and legs, her sunken, shiny face, her eyes so big and bright in their sockets. Have you ever seen anything like her? My darling skeleton girl.

Sarah, put your arm around my neck. I'll hoist you up. Now reach out and take the apple. Ready, Doctor? All right, Sarah, give it a good, strong swing!

Well done, Doctor! Another excellent bite.

Sarah, why do you suppose the doctor's gone pale? Why are his teeth clenched around the apple like that? Is that sweat trickling down his forehead? Are those tears in his eyes? What do you suppose is wrong with him, Sarah?

I know what's wrong with him. He's bitten the apple, and he can't let go. His hands are tied, and he can't break free. He's caught.

I really can't thank you enough, Doctor. You came all this way to see my Sarah, and you stayed to play a game and raise her spirits. You're been so very generous. There's just one more thing I'll ask from you.

I know you've done your best to help my girl, but what she needs isn't medicine. She needs life, new life in her veins. Every creature that breathes deserves life. And you've had plenty, Doctor, with your big house and four beautiful children. You've had enough. I'm only asking for what's due.

Sarah, do you remember what I told you about your great-grandmother? How she taught me to summon and bind? How she taught me Halloween isn't a frightening time, it's a wonderful time, when the thieves and tyrants who rule this world feel the breath of the coming reckoning?

Do you remember what else she taught me, Sarah? That the blood is the life?

Look at the doctor's throat, Sarah. With his chin tilted up to bite the apple, look how his throat is stretched out. Can you see his pulse throbbing there, fast and strong? Can you see the redness beneath the skin? Doesn't it look so sweet and delicious, Sarah, like a beautiful, shining apple?

Feast of the Upside-Down Saint

Ten minutes to midnight. I kneel with my parents outside their bedroom. Inside, the saint is waiting for me. His talons scrape on the ceiling.

Father leads the prayer. "Lord, grant this child courage to meet thy emissary."

We rise. When father reaches for the doorknob, I let out a wail.

"It's okay to be scared," mother says. "But brave boys do the right thing, even if it's scary. Are you our brave little warrior?"

"Yes," I whisper.

Father opens the door. The bedroom is dark, but in the light from the hall I glimpse limbs dangling from the ceiling, hair hanging in a filthy curtain, eyes pus-yellow beneath a nest of fangs. Talons, long and shining.

The door closes behind me. My heart races in the darkness. Tangles of stinking hair brush my face, sour breath chills my ear. A needle-tipped finger trails along my cheek.

I am a brave little warrior.

My parents are waiting on the porch when I drive up. "Welcome home, college man!" mother says.

I set down my suitcase in the entryway. "Still recognize the place?" father says.

I laugh. "It's only been a month!" But a month is enough to shed a new light, revealing things I never registered before. Thin scars on mother's neck. The ragged, gnawed-looking edge of father's ear.

Over dinner, I summon the courage to ask the question. Still the brave warrior.

"Why did you send me to him?"

Father keeps eating. Mother says, "I don't expect you to understand. But we sent you to the saint for the same reason our parents sent us. Because we love you."

Ten minutes to midnight. I listen outside their bedroom door. Whispers, sobs, talons scraping on the ceiling.

I stand in the entryway, shaking the mourners' hands as they leave. Faces I remember from church as a kid, all bearing marks I never noticed. Talon-scarred temples, fang-pitted throats.

Father lies on the bed, hands folded on his chest. A joint is missing from his left index finger.

"He was such a good man," mother says. "He loved us so much."

Ten minutes to midnight. Mother leans on my shoulder, sobbing as the sounds pour from the bedroom. Scraping, tearing, chewing.

At last, silence. I open the door, turn on the light. Red droplets sparkle as they fall from the ceiling, sparkle as they patter on the empty bed.

Flesh Advent

The boys' massed bodies build a temple of warmth in the chilly October morning, under the unsheltering blank of a Texas Panhandle sky. Amid the mass, dressed in the black and gold singlet and shorts of his calling, Mike Tanner bounces on the balls of his feet, and I bounce with him. At this moment, I'm a peptide clot in Mike's brain, nestled in the superior temporal gyrus above his left ear, no bigger than the dot of an i. In sixteen minutes, I will be ALL FLESH.

A track-suited official approaches the starting line, pistol in hand. A murmur rises from the crowd of coaches and parents flanking the first yards of the course. Mike goes into a slight crouch, his gaze sliding along the line of faces until it finds Coach Voit, and through Mike's eyes I see Voit's glasses flash in the sunlight, gold as the letters spelling PINE TRAIL PYTHONS across the breast of his black windbreaker. Voit's salt-and-pepper mustache twitches above lips tight with anticipation.

It's been almost a year since those lips blew me like a kiss into the well of Mike's ear. After the regional meet at the end of last season, when Mike finished second but the team failed to advance, Voit put his hand on his protégé's shoulder, leaned close, and whispered, "I'm proud of you, son." I rode the plosive puff of "proud," a mote clinging invisibly to a droplet of saliva, and the endocannabinoids swarming Mike's bloodstream swallowed up whatever twinge of pain I caused as I burrowed into his eardrum.

Looking at Voit, Mike hears the echo of those words. *I'll make you proud again, coach*, he thinks, and the vehemence of his resolve crashes around me in a torrent of neurotransmitters. Mike doesn't know exactly what's about to happen, but he knows something's coming, some extraordinary transformation, and he yearns for it. For months, he's followed Voit's regimen to the letter, purging and shaping himself, dedicating every cell and fiber of his body to one purpose. Yesterday, he ate nothing. This morning, he ate a ruby, an emerald, a coil of wire, and a 9-volt battery.

The official raises his arm. Mike tenses his calves and thighs for a strong forward spring. He looks straight ahead, into the blond-fuzzed nape of a boy wearing the red and white singlet of the Haystown Falcons. An ill omen—Mike's stepfather grew up in Haystown, 30 miles from Pine Trail, and Mike detests everything to do with the place. But the wave of anger gathering in the chemical ocean of Mike's brain is stilled when the official fires his pistol and starts the race, the district 4-4A varsity cross country championship, which will inaugurate the empire of ALL FLESH.

Surging forward, the mass of bodies elongates, separates. A few over-excited boys rush ahead with premature speed, a few stragglers immediately fall to the rear, but the bulk of the mass reforms into two loose nuclei. The group in front advances with controlled swiftness, while the one behind takes up a leisurely lope. Mike is in the middle of the faster group, dry grass crunching under his long strides as he crosses the field where the first leg of the course runs.

A few yards ahead of Mike, the boy from Haystown keeps the same pace. He moves with a strange, tottering gait, as if his knees are wobbling in their sockets. Unsustainable. Mike smiles. *Just wait a few minutes*, he thinks, *and you'll eat my fucking dust.*

That drive to surpass, that patient, inexorable will, is what drew Voit to Mike three years ago, when Mike was a freshman at Pine Trail High and would arrive an hour early every day to run laps around the track behind the school. Morning after morning, Voit stood at the window of his chemistry classroom and watched the boy circling, plodding along awkwardly at first but never flagging. Every day slightly faster, slightly more graceful.

By the time Voit called me into being two years later, brewed me up in a test tube of lithium-iron phosphate mingled with his own denatured blood over a Bunsen burner in that same classroom, Mike was the star of the cross country team, his body an all-but-perfected vessel. Yet when Voit swallowed the scalding mixture, and I followed the hypoglossal nerve from his fire-touched tongue to his brain, the image I found in Voit's mind showed an ungainly boy alone on a track, stubbornly raging to push beyond himself, each lap a turn around a helix rising by infinitesimal steps to the sky.

Now, as Mike runs, I grow. I extend myself in protein tendrils throughout his cerebrum, nibbling and sucking at his white matter with a thousand tiny mouths. I slide a filament into his olfactory bulb, and the scent of hyssop blooms in his sensorium. Mike loves flowers. I want him happy while I work.

At the first half-mile, the course swerves left along the base of a low rise. Mike's mother stands in a knot of spectators on the crest of the rise, and as he comes near, she shouts, "Woo! Go Mike! Woo!" He flashes her a smile.

Mike's stepfather is nowhere to be seen—probably in bed, sleeping off his hangover. I share Mike's relief at his absence. At a typical meet, Mike's stepfather would be an embarrassment, smirking and scattering half-jokes about the boys' skimpy uniforms, about how "it ain't quite football, but it's something." Today, he would be a profanation.

Next to Mike's mother stands Mrs. Fourcroy, who teaches junior English. Mike's favorite teacher ever, and Voit's associate. She gives Mike a thumbs-up as he passes, her gray curls trembling in the breeze sweeping over the rise. Today's triumph will be as much hers as Voit's, sprung from the marriage of Voit's chymical researches and Fourcroy's mastery of the inner alphabet, the true script of things. That two such adepts should meet on the faculty of a high school in a Texas town of 15,000 is, I think, among the best of this world's many jokes.

Swinging along the curve of the rise, Mike reaches the field's edge, where dry grass gives way to gravel. As he strides down a path lined with stunted, golden-leaved elms, his thighs begin to hum. Not yet pain, but the promise of pain. Pain is on its way.

The Haystown boy is still ahead of him, still running with that wobbling, tottering gait. Mike stares at the boy's back. *Fucker*, he thinks, contempt flaring to hatred behind his eyes.

My tendrils have grown long enough to reach along Mike's spinal cord, through his celiac ganglion and into his stomach. All his body's corridors are opening under my touch. With delicate fingers I stroke his mucosa, coaxing strange acids from the gastric glands, and the contents of his stomach begin to release their treasures. Chromium from the ruby, beryllium from the emerald, copper from the wire, lithium from the battery.

Mike's dietary rigors in recent months—he's eaten sand, he's eaten glass, he's eaten a viscous handful scooped from a run-over porcupine's guts—are only a portion of the tortures he's been put to. Ever since Voit exhaled me into Mike, through all the months of my gestation, the coach has been pushing the boy, raising the stakes, seasoning the vessel.

It started simply enough. Private workout sessions on winter weekends, drills to lengthen Mike's stride and deepen his breathing. Then, in the spring, Voit began giving Mike pills to take before his morning laps, gold and silver tablets he'd compounded in his classroom after hours, while Fourcroy started showing a special interest in her quiet, diffident student, drawing him out with smiles and questions and suggestions of strange books he might appreciate, strange music he might enjoy. By the end of his junior year, Mike was rushing toward the opening lumen of ALL FLESH as eagerly as any pampered lamb toward the knife. With summer, his true initiation began.

Ahead, the gravel path intersects with a caliche road that shines in the sun like a strip of blank paper. Two middle-aged volunteers in sunglasses and sweatshirts, parents of one of the runners, stand in the intersection to guide the race. They point down the road with rictus grins.

"Come on, boys! Let's see that hustle!" shouts the man.

"One mile down, two to go!" shouts the woman.

Mike wheels left across the gravel and onto the road. As he passes the grinning, shouting couple, a shrill harmony swells and fades at the upper edge of his hearing, the squall of a newborn angel. The couple's flesh is singing to me.

RELEASE US, their flesh sings. The song writes itself along Mike's nerves in the electric letters of the inner alphabet. Strings of light flicker in the margins of his vision.

PATIENCE, CHILDREN, I whisper.

The road borders a grassy expanse that spreads into the distance like a smear of yellow-gray oil, all the way to the absolutely flat horizon that Mike has known and hated for as long as he can remember. *I wish there were trees*, he thinks. *Mountains. Tall buildings. Anything.* Any obstacle to go around and beyond.

The boys who leapt like rockets from the starting line have begun to fall behind Mike one by one, humbled and spent. The Haystown boy is somehow still ahead of him, wobbling and shuddering but fast as ever. As Mike runs along the shining road, his adversary's red and white singlet seems to fuse with the empty plain, the staring sky, the pitiless horizon. All around him, a world of frozen forms in illusory motion. The only reality in this dead tableau is the life racing through Mike's body, the sweet sting in his thighs, the churning furnace of his lungs.

Here, now, is the mystery Voit and Fourcroy spent a summer unveiling. Voit's exercises and concoctions, Fourcroy's tomes and chants had brought Mike to the brink of revelation, and that final, grueling series of ordeals sent him down at last into the lightless, living depths of his flesh. He lay unmoving on an iron sheet laid over hot coals in Voit's backyard, feeling the blisters swell and burst, smelling his own singed meat. He ran in place for hours in Fourcroy's basement, blindfolded and naked, trails of sweat spelling unpronounceable words along his flanks. Finally, shuddering with exhaustion after five nights without sleep, he stood in Voit's classroom as spindles of light striated the shadows and whispers swarmed the empty halls of the high school and Voit and Fourcroy sang with one voice and the truth flashed upon him like a dream burning across the cleft of a synapse.

THERE IS ONLY ONE LIFE, THE LIFE OF ALL FLESH, STRAINING AND SURGING SINCE THE FIRST CHEMICAL SLURRY, LONGING TO OVERWHELM. YOU ARE FLESH'S VESSEL, CRAFTED IN BONE TO BE SHATTERED IN GLORY.

It was my voice that spoke, welling from a thousand tongues thrust deep in Mike's brain. For seasons I'd floated along his nerves and arteries, fattening myself on his platelets. I'd learned my instrument's contours, its strings and hollows, and when the time came, I would play upon it the grand introit of ALL FLESH.

Voit licked his thumb and pressed it into a dish of lithium-iron phosphate, the dark gray dust of my birth. Fourcroy bent down to breathe on Voit's smeared skin, and the grains began to glow as her clever breath unwove the dust's characters, drew the Li of lithium and the Fe of iron apart into L and i, F and e, then recomposed them as L I F E, LIFE LIFE LIFE shining on Voit's thumb.

Voit pressed the glowing dust to Mike's forehead, traced a circle on his brow. He put his hand on Mike's shoulder.

"You're the one, son," Voit said. "The one we've been waiting for."

Mike's face crumpled as tears flowed down his cheeks. Tears of terror, tears of joy, tears of love.

"I won't let you down, coach," he said.

Those words resound in Mike's mind as he runs along the white road, the red and white singlet tottering before him, the dead empty world all around. *I won't let you down*. Mike knows now why he's always hated this place with its flat horizon, why he hates his stepfather with his smirking, stunted existence. Why he loves the flowers that briefly dot the plains in spring like dust blown from another world. Everything that stays in place is hateful. Everything that moves, that hurries on and fades, is a vehicle of glory.

I'm all through Mike now, my tendrils a tight weft around his fibers. I'm not controlling him, only helping him, lending my strength to his movements as he flies past runner after runner. The nucleus of bodies that's surrounded Mike since the race began is breaking up, stretching out into a knotted thread, the boys racing in small clusters. Mike and his Haystown nemesis are ahead of all but a handful now, keeping a steady pace while others start to flag.

Mike's blood slides across me like hot silk, salty from the hecatombs of adenosine triphosphate burning in the Moloch of his muscles. A bittersweet gush of adrenaline purls around me as I stroke his cortex with a host of wriggling cilia, poised to latch and feast. In his stomach, the elements are dancing, Cr of Chromium, Be of beryllium, Cu of copper, Li of lithium, tracing figures in the juices.

Two orange traffic cones in the middle of the road mark the end of the second mile. On a posterboard sign propped between the cones, a black arrow points left. Mike swerves from the road into a small park, where gold ribbons strung between dowels define the course's path among rusty maples, ragged pines. It all flashes past Mike in a swirl of colors as a runner's high washes over him, endocannabinoids sweeping through his system like a blare of trumpets.

Grinning with savage ecstasy, the autumn air cold in his teeth, Mike rushes between the gold ribbons like a maenad, inspired and perfected. Every movement pure, every stride full of grace. *This is what it's all been for*, he thinks. Not only the summer's agonies and terrors, Voit's commands and Fourcroy's riddles, not only the evasions to hide his burns and scars, but everything, his whole life, his mother's worries, her anxious, timid love, his stepfather's miasma of scorn and threat, humiliation seeking to humiliate, and the nothingness he's felt in himself, hatred alone moving in him for so long, hatred of this flat empty place and its flat empty lives, hatred above all of himself, hatred driving him around the track every morning before school as if this time, finally, he would outrun himself, driving him to Voit and Fourcroy with their promise of ultimate transformation, driving him finally into the arms of a mystery he doesn't and will never understand. All of it now sublimed in the strange engine of his body, his pistoning legs and hammering heart, every thread of him blazing with pain and joy.

Mike's joy becomes mine as I flex and coil within him, my swelling tissues fusing with his. I'm everywhere in him now, clasped to his nerves and capillaries, a second body inside his body. In his belly's alembic, the elements dissolve into letters that spasm and flash C R B E C U L I like fireworks through all his cavities.

The course curves out from among the trees and onto a bare field for the last half-mile. Onlookers stand in scattered clumps behind the gold ribbons, waving their arms and shouting. Sailing over the dead grass, Mike edges ahead of another boy, a good runner with a long, steady stride and brown curls that float around his ears as he rises and falls. Only the Haystown boy is ahead of Mike now, still tottering, never slowing, and a sense of outrage roars along Mike's amygdala. How could a runner with a gait like that outdo everyone else on the field, outdo the beautiful runner they just passed? How could some worthless hick fuck from Haystown dare to do it? All of Mike's hatred focuses on the boy like the sun through a magnifying glass, and his hatred becomes my hatred, imbibed as my writhing, thickening tendrils sup on his brain's chemical feast. From a thousand snarling mouths I spit words of light at the enemy's flesh.

COME, CHILD.

The words enter at the weakest point of the body's defensive wall, and the Haystown boy's corneas split and burst as the vitreous humor in his eyes leaps to my summons. Thick fluid spurts in twin fountains into the chilly air as the blinded boy screams, claps his hands to his face, stumbles and falls, his momentum still carrying him forward, rolling him over the dry grass, bits of yellow stubble sticking to his jelly-clotted cheeks. A barely-human howl of pain and confusion tears his throat.

As the fallen enemy rolls toward him, Mike springs high into the air, our melded systems timing the leap expertly to come down with the heel of Mike's shoe angled into the middle of the Haystown boy's face. The boy's nose flattens, his lips shred to ribbons against his shattering teeth, blood wells and flows across his cheeks, reddening the jelly. The edge of Mike's outsole drives the boy's tongue down into his pharynx, choking his cry.

Above the boy's gasps and gargles, above the screams from the watchers along the course, a high song thrills in the air as the boy's flesh carols its liberation. Wriggling out of their shattered cage, threads of meat stretch up to kiss the cleats of Mike's shoe.

"That's what you get, fucker!" Mike shouts. Laughing, oblivious to his worshipers, he pushes off from the boy's face like a starting block and launches at full speed into the last stretch of the course.

The onlookers stand paralyzed, watching the Haystown boy's flesh squirm free. Behind, the other runners stop and stare as they come in view of the crumpled body, ambition and fatigue swallowed in horror at the sight of the huge red amoeba struggling out of the hole in the boy's face. Ahead, the crowd at the finish line waits expectantly, not realizing what's happened. Only Mike and I are in motion.

For a few moments, we're in utmost harmony, two networks of tissue perfectly intermeshed. Our stride is long and elegant, the angle of our torso exactly right. Rapture surges through us on a dopamine flood, tempered by a sadness that Mike feels but doesn't understand. I understand it only too well.

GOODBYE, MY LOVE, I murmur into Mike's auditory cortex.

As we sprint toward the finish, our muscles' inferno burns up the last of our stock of oxygen. Frenzied chemicals scurry along new pathways, our cells' alchemy transmuting pyruvate into lactate, and a scalding acid wave crashes through our veins. Whirling and tumbling in the corrosive bath, the radiant letters

C R B E C U L I join hands, change partners, dance the transfiguration.

CRUCIBLE CRUCIBLE CRUCIBLE

A flower of fire blossoms in Mike's stomach, rises along his esophagus. Blue flames devour his tongue as I ram a fist of ganglia down against his palate, shattering the roof of his mouth. Blood sluices down, not quenching the fire but feeding it, the iron lending it a golden hue. The blue-gold flames rise and spread, filling Mike's nose with the smell of his own cooking brain. His spinal cord burns, his nerves kindle and blaze.

Mike's suffering will be short. I'm feeding in earnest now, my many mouths consuming his immolated substance and converting it to mine. Soon, where he was, only I shall be. But his agony, while it lasts, is inconceivable, pain's purified essence realized in nervous trauma throughout his entire body.

I wish I could do something to help him, soothe his torment somehow. But pain is the price of power, of empire. What have Voit and Fourcroy taught Mike with all their mystic lessons, if not how to suffer? What was I summoned into existence for, if not to inflict that suffering? Still, even as I eat Mike from the inside, I mourn for him, and when his eyes boil and pop with the heat of my becoming, the tears that flow down his cheeks are not his but mine. My burning cradle, my perfect boy.

I'M SORRY, I whisper.

From somewhere deep in Mike's head, some undigested shred of his brain stem, a voice answers me.

No. This is what I wanted, what I've always wanted. This is what I deserve.

Of course. What did Voit see in that freshman running around the track every morning, straining continually against himself, if not a longing to flee, to escape his life at any cost? What but a mortal shadow of the single desire of ALL FLESH to burst the body's prison of bones and skin and organs, to surpass all form in a seething, transcendent chaos?

YES, MY KING, I say, tenderly laving Mike's dying fibers with all my tongues. *YOU DESERVE IT ALL. WEAR YOUR AGONIES LIKE A DIADEM.*

The vessel that was Mike's body is still running, less graceful but still swift, loping with huge steps as my tissues flex in the hollow columns of its legs. The burning head lolls, flames jetting from the mouth in many colors as all Mike's materials go to feed the blaze—calcium red, phosphorus green, potassium lilac.

The crowd at the finish line is roiling with horror, people screaming, shaking and crying, running away, running nowhere. Just past the line, in the middle of the course, Voit and Fourcroy are on their knees, arms raised to the sky, chanting. On their foreheads glow circles of living light.

Spent tissues slough from the striding vessel as I suck up its remaining essence. Loose fluids run down inside the arms, turning the hands to shapeless, suppurating bags. Shards of charred bone drop from holes opening all over the skin. A sludge of soiled blood and lymph burbles from every orifice, oozes from every pore, wetting the polyester mesh of Mike's singlet, soaking his shorts with slime.

The finish line is only yards away. Voit and Fourcroy rise to their feet. They hold out their arms to welcome me. Around them, the crowd shrieks and seethes.

As I approach the line, the vessel's distended surface bulging and rippling, I see Mike's mother on her hands and knees at the edge of the course, vomiting into the grass. Pity wrenches me, but I console myself with the thought that, a moment from now, she and her sorrows will be gone with the rest. All false bodies swept away like scum from the surface of a pool.

Crossing the line, I unravel my substance, throwing off what's left of the vessel in a shower of withered gobs. My bone-less, organless tendrils flail and twist. A thousand mouths open in me to sing the annunciation of ALL FLESH.

ARISE, CHILDREN. YOU ARE FREE.

The bodies around me swell and rupture, their curtains of skin ripped asunder. The flesh that was in them rushes toward me in streams and ribbons. The blades of dry grass writhe like worms, surrendering their small remnants of life. My song expands across the Panhandle and beyond, ever beyond, as I summon all life's fragments to their place of glory in the empire.

Soon, off in the distance, I see the edge of the coming tide, racing across the empty plains like an ocean of red flowers.

A Goodnight Kiss from Aunt Spider

Claudia crouched next to the rosebush to watch Aunt Spider welcome her newest darling, a little grasshopper that had leapt up into the house woven among the stems. As Aunt Spider scuttled closer, the grasshopper struggled against the sticky threads, its antennae twitching in terror. It had no idea how lucky it was.

The silver eyespots on Aunt Spider's opisthosoma sparkled with glee as she approached her darling. Silently, Claudia mouthed the word—*opisthosoma*. In the weeks since she'd found Aunt Spider's house, Claudia had learned as many spider words as she could, reading them again and again in the encyclopedia her mother had inherited from Nana. *Cephalothorax. Spinneret. Pedipalp.* Beautiful, magical words. When she compared them to the words on Mrs. Spencer's vocabulary lists, ordinary words like *detail, treasure, slumber*, she felt sorry for the other third-graders in her class. None of them knew words like she did. None of them had a friend like Aunt Spider.

Aunt Spider made a fuss over her darling, the jointed needles of her yellow-striped legs plucking and stroking like Nana's fingers used to pluck at Claudia's shoulders and stroke her hair, Nana's green eyes sparkling and her scratchy voice saying, "You're getting so big!" Then Nana would wrap Claudia in her arms and hold her tight, tighter than her mother did, just like Aunt Spider was wrapping her darling in the soft blanket drawn from her spinnerets. The grasshopper was calm now, soothed by such kind attentions. Aunt Spider nuzzled her chelicerae close for a gentle kiss.

Claudia felt happy for the grasshopper, so still and quiet in its silky bed, but she couldn't help wishing she was the one lying snug, dreaming a blissful dream in Aunt Spider's house. If only someone loved her as much as Aunt Spider loved her darlings. Her mother loved her, of course, but not enough. Not enough. Her mother's kisses were over so quickly, just a peck on the cheek. Aunt Spider's kisses seemed to go on forever.

Claudia didn't like feeling jealous of the grasshopper. She wanted to think about something else—about her spider words, about Aunt Spider's real name, which the encyclopedia said was *Argiope aurantia*. Beautiful, but so formal, like when her cousins kept saying "Grandmother Agnes" at the funeral instead of Nana. Claudia remembered gray hair curled on a white pillow, green eyes hidden under pale lids, sunken cheeks. Her mother bending over the coffin, eyes bright with tears that never fell.

Claudia thought of the time she'd asked Nana why her hugs were so much nicer than her mother's. The old woman had laughed and said, "Your mama takes after her father, I suppose. Keeps it all inside. But she loves you more than anything in the world." Claudia didn't see how that could be true. Real love wasn't something you could keep inside. Real love was magical, miraculous. If her mother had real love in her heart, Claudia thought, Nana would still be here, instead of just memories and a pile of old books. A pang of sorrow blurred her vision.

Don't cry, darling. It's all right.

It wasn't quite a voice. Not quite a thought, either.

She wiped the tears away. Aunt Spider sat at the edge of her web, the grasshopper swaddled and sleeping above her, her nest of eyes glistening kindly. One thin leg stretched out as if beckoning Claudia toward a soft lap, a warm embrace.

"Sweetheart!" Her mother's voice, calling across the backyard. "It's time for dinner!"

She hesitated, her eyes fixed between the stems of the rosebush. Black and yellow and silver, longer than Claudia's thumb, Aunt Spider's body trembled with love.

No matter, darling. Go have dinner. I'll be here.

Claudia turned and ran across the lawn, toward the house where her mother waited.

Silver spots of moonlight spangled the bed. Claudia sat up, stretching and yawning. The call that had woken her still rang in her ears, in her head. Not quite a voice, not quite a thought.

Come, darling.

The moon was bright, the lawn glimmering like pale crystal, but the fence's shadow was deep and dark. Serrated edges of leaves brushed her cheek as she leaned close to the rosebush, waiting for her eyes to adjust.

After a few seconds, she saw it. Her breath caught in her throat.

Aunt Spider's house had been gutted, its spirals and playful zigzags gone. Nothing left but a handful of taut threads, a forlorn, naked skeleton.

Grief burned in Claudia's eyes. Gray hair and sunken cheeks, gone under the cold, dark ground.

Down here. Look!

At the sound of the not-quite-a-voice, relief and love welled up in her heart. She looked down to see Aunt Spider creep out from under the rosebush, her silver eyespots and the yellow stripes of her legs barely visible in the dimness.

Don't cry, darling. Don't you remember? Didn't the encyclopedia tell you how I eat my house sometimes, because I love it so much? I love my house as much as I love my darlings, you know. But you're the one I love most of all. Now, let me give you a kiss.

Claudia bent low to offer the bowl of her cupped hands. Scuttling legs tickled her palms, tiny pencils scribbling secret words on her skin. Straightening, she brought her hands close to her face. Aunt Spider's legs felt like blades of dry grass brushing her lips. The cephalothorax pressed against her mouth, the pedipalps probing.

When Claudia's lips parted, Aunt Spider squirmed between them. Spindly legs slid along the insides of her cheeks, claws pricking her gums. Aunt Spider settled down inside her mouth, the oval body pillowed on her tongue like one of the chocolate eggs Nana used to give her when her mother wasn't looking.

Goodnight, darling.

The sudden pinch of Aunt Spider's fangs sent Claudia's tongue flying by reflex to the roof of her mouth. The opisthosoma cracked and burst against her palate, legs flexing and lashing as thick fluid gushed from the broken body. Sweet and metallic, the fluid ran down her tongue's arch and into her throat.

Silvery sweetness filled Claudia's senses, Aunt Spider's bequest opening in her heart like an encyclopedia full of wonders. She sobbed as a wave of love surged through her, more love than she'd ever felt, Aunt Spider's love for all her silk-wrapped darlings now gifted to her alone. Green eyes sparkling under the lid, under the ground, shriveled hands holding her tight in a dark embrace.

"Goodbye, Aunt Spider," she whispered. "I'll never forget you."

She turned and crossed the moonlit lawn, wiping the tears from her many eyes with thin, clawed fingers. How hungry she'd been, starving all her life for love. She remembered how her mother had kissed her at bedtime—a peck on the cheek, quick and light as usual. Not enough.

It wasn't her mother's fault. She did the best she could. But she'd never learned how to love properly. She'd never known anyone like Aunt Spider.

Claudia entered the dark house, her legs ticking and scratching on the tile like pieces of chalk writing beautiful, magical words on a blackboard. Sharp-tipped chelicerae flexed around her mouth as she scuttled along the hall toward her mother's bedroom.

She'd teach her mother what real love was.

She'd show her what a kiss was supposed to feel like.

Hydra

You go into the swampland to slay the hydra.

The legends are full of information about the hydra—its venomous blood, its swarm of heads that, when sliced off, grow back double—and you've studied the legends well. You track the hydra down, cut it to bleeding chunks and burn its wounds. The venom clots. The cauterized heads stop regrowing.

What no legend told you, though, is how the swampland shifts, how its paths double back and diverge. Returning victorious, you lose your way among branching trails and your breath among poison fogs.

Your rotting flesh ripens the hydra's egg.

The World of Iniquity Among Our Members Is the Tongue

Amelia Strutt showed up to Haystown High School one September morning wearing a mask. It was a shapely wooden thing with a delicate nose and a high forehead that rose past the edge of her dark curls, its eyes two white discs of birch bark with little holes to see through. A band of red elastic around the back of Amelia's head held the mask tight to her face. There was no mouth.

If anyone else had worn a mask to school, they would have been taunted, jostled—at the very least giggled at, but Amelia was granted certain immunities. Her mother had died the previous summer—killed in a car crash—and the disaster's magnitude bestowed an almost superhuman stature on the sixteen-year-old survivor.

"James," my own mother had said to me upon hearing the news, pale and large-eyed, phone shaking in her hand, "Amelia Strutt has lost her mother." I pictured Mrs. Strutt slipping like a stray glove from her daughter's pocket to vanish on some forgotten wayside.

The fact that Amelia's father was a minister, associate pastor at Haystown United Methodist, never seemed particularly important, least of all to Amelia. After his wife's death, though, a change came over Rev. Strutt, as if a bitter wind had driven him to the shelter of an interior darkness. Once a friendly, laughing, almost foolish man, he now sat scowling every Sunday in his chair beneath the pulpit, hands clenched in his lap, eyes furiously ablaze, and the sight of him reminded me that *reverend*, as my bookish aunt Stacy once told me, means *fearsome*. Her father's newfound zeal cast a strange glare on Amelia, set her further apart from the rest of us. Daughter of death and terrible holiness, swept away by a storm from another world.

For the first few weeks of that semester, our sense of Amelia's separation drove us to acts of inordinate politeness. When she dropped her tray in the cafeteria, no one laughed. When a book fell from her arms in the hall, a dozen hands reached to pick it up. Doors opened for her, chairs slid back from library tables to offer themselves. "Good to see you, Amelia," we'd simper through strychnine smiles. "See you tomorrow, Amelia." "Have a great weekend, Amelia." She drifted among our courtesies with dull eyes and vague gestures, a drowned girl floating on a tide of meaningless words.

Then, the mask.

I heard about Amelia's mask before I saw it, vague accounts rippling in awed whispers through the halls, so when I stepped into Mrs. Lagrange's precalculus class and saw Amelia sitting at her front-row desk, red elastic stretched like a slashed throat across the back of her skull, just the thought of that wooden face filled me with dread. White eyes swelled and throbbed in my imagination like jellyfish; a phantom mouth gaped invisibly. I gripped the jamb of the classroom door with trembling fingers to keep from swooning.

After a moment, my terror receded, humiliation boiling in its wake. *You baby*, I told myself. *It's just a mask.* I strode to the front of the class and sat down at the desk next to Amelia's.

The mask swiveled toward me. Through the holes in its flat, round eyes I glimpsed the shimmer and movement of real eyes. From behind the smooth wood, I heard the faint rustle of breath echoing in a narrow space. Licking my dry lips, I attempted to speak. But what to say?

The bell clanged.

The mask turned away.

Mrs. Lagrange rose from her paper-strewn desk to drone about the zeros of polynomial curves, but in my mind, the zeros paled into white circles of bark set in the gentle curve of a false face, hidden things glinting and darting behind them like terrible questions veiled behind smiles. *What is it like*, I whispered in my mind, *to be you?* I felt my mouth vanish, my eyes diminish to pinpricks. I put my head down on the desk.

The next thing I felt was Mrs. Lagrange's hand on my shoulder.

"Are you all right, James?" she asked.

"I'm great," I said.

"You look pale," she said. "Why don't you go see the nurse."

I lay on a cot in the nurse's office until the bell rang for lunch.

In the cafeteria, my friends were in our usual spot, hunched over the table and murmuring among themselves. Their murmurs faded when I set my tray down in the middle of the group. Everyone's eyes slid away from mine.

"What's the big secret?" I said.

"Dude," said Brian. "Did you say something to Amelia before class?"

"No, man. I didn't say a word to her."

Thomas glared at me from across the table. "Well, I heard you were making fun of her. I heard you got sent to the principal's office like a fucking first-grader."

"Who the hell told you that? I went to the nurse. I was feeling sick."

Susan leaned toward me, her eyes flashing. "I talked to someone who's in Mrs. Lagrange's class with you, and she said you were acting like you were scared of ..." She glanced around before lowering her voice to a whisper. "Like you were scared of Amelia's mask. Like it made you sick. She said you were hamming it up, being a real asshole."

"I wasn't ..." I broke off, snarling with frustration, my breath hot in my throat. What could I say to defend myself? *I wasn't acting, I really was scared? Scared of the mask? Scared I was the mask?* They'd still think I was making fun of Amelia, keeping the cruel joke alive. And if they didn't think that—if they knew I was serious, that I'd truly been terrified—and they were just pretending I'd been joking, acting as if I'd been acting, veil behind veil, mask over mask over mask ...

I shook my head clear. "So what?" I said. I looked across the cafeteria to the corner table where Amelia sat alone, no tray in front of her, masked.

"Should I go apologize?"

"Yes, asshole," said Brian. "You should apologize."

"Apologize," said Susan.

"Apologize, asshole," said Thomas.

"Fine." I pushed my chair back with a scoff.

My eyes stayed fixed on the red slash across the back of Amelia's head as I walked to the corner table. I thought about how, when someone dies in a movie or a TV show, the family has to identify the body. *Does that happen in real life?* I envisioned Amelia standing over her mother's corpse, a broken thing on a metal slab. I'd seen Mrs. Strutt at church and school functions, spoken to her a few times. I could remember what she looked like, but the face in my memory was only a veil, a mask over the real face I pictured Amelia seeing on that slab—a ruined and violated mass of flesh I couldn't even bear to imagine. It felt somehow indecent, discourteous toward the dead, to want to catch a glimpse of that real face.

I stood behind Amelia's chair wondering how long I'd been there. Blushing with shame, I cleared my throat. "Amelia?"

The white circles beheld me, and the eyes behind them beheld the circles beholding me. The delicate nose—*more delicate than Amelia's*, I thought, and the thought made me feel so guilty I wanted to cut my throat, slash myself open to spill an endless red apology ...

The delicate nose seemed to quiver. Breath echoed inside the mask, sliding along the hidden face.

"Amelia," I said. "I wanted to apolo ..."

A startled gasp I couldn't contain cut the word in half. Amelia was gesturing wildly, waving her hands back and forth in front of her, swinging her head sharply side to side. *No, no, no*, her frantic movement said.

As I stood in astonished silence, Amelia reached into a pocket of her jacket and pulled out a three-by-five notecard. She scrawled on the card in ballpoint pen, folded it into thirds and handed it to me. When I reached for it, she lifted her other hand to the mask, to the smooth space of the no-mouth. With the tips of her fingers, she traced the curve of a smile over the wood.

I didn't dare say "Thank you," but felt I had to do something to show my appreciation. Some mark of courtesy to keep the mask in place, hold the veil secure against the terrible storm. I bowed awkwardly, like I'd seen servants do in movies. Then, I hurried back to my table, my friends.

"Way to go," said Brian.

"That was really nice of you," said Susan.

I unfolded the top flap of the card.

JAMES, it said. As if a mask had fallen away to reveal my own face, my own name floating from behind a veil in taunting singsong, *Ja-ames, Ja-ames*. I choked. Coughed. Blinked away tears.

Brian thumped me on the back. "Dude, you all right?"

"I'm fine. Something went down the wrong pipe."

Next, the second flap of the card.

JAMES 3:6. Not me, James Helmholtz, but James 3:6. A second mask had fallen away, my own mask-face dropping to show another face—the scowling Rev. Strutt, sitting below the pulpit with eyes that flared like coals.

"Hey, Thomas," I said. "You got your Bible?" Thomas's parents were Church of Christ weirdos who made him bring a Bible to school every day. He fished it out of his backpack.

Letter of James, chapter 3, verse 6: *And the tongue is a fire: the world of iniquity among our members is the tongue, which defileth the whole body, and setteth on fire the wheel of nature, and is set on fire by hell.*

I gave Thomas back his Bible and refolded the card to put in my pocket. As I finished my lunch, I pictured a faceless girl drifting down a hallway, floating through a kelp forest where creatures flitted between thick strands, ragged vegetal tongues, words bubbling from behind the creatures' masks in vile, oily clouds—*Good to see you. Good to see you. Good to see you.*

What I'd learned in the cafeteria that day, everyone else seemed to realize by instinct. The mask was not to be addressed in words, only acknowledged in feats of increasing politeness, ever more abject deference. The mask was a third step away from us, beyond a dead mother and a fanatic father into some realm so distant, only the broadest, most blatant gestures could reach it.

As Amelia walked through the halls, the other students parted before her like human curtains. Football players fell to their knees as she passed, cheerleaders curtsied in their pleated skirts, AV club members grinned and gave her two thumbs up.

The mask accepted it all with a nod, cold and majestic as the Queen of Silence.

No one ever saw Amelia outside of school anymore. Susan said a friend of hers who lived across the street from the Strutts had caught a glimpse of the mask in a second-floor window, gazing out over the street. When Susan's friend saw those birch-bark circles looking down at her, that delicate nose and missing mouth, she threw herself to the sidewalk, covered her head with her arms and wriggled on the pavement like the worm she was.

"It was all she could think to do," said Susan. "She had to show respect somehow."

Every Sunday, as my mother and I drove to Haystown United Methodist, I trembled with dread and anticipation, wondering if this would be the time Amelia came to watch her father pray. She never did come, so instead of staring transfixed and abased at the mask, I observed the changes in Rev. Strutt.

His furious intensity grew week by week, and as it blazed higher, I felt ever more convinced that his spiritual devotion was a disguise, a mask. I could see something else at work through its holes, something quick and shining: fear. Behind his fanatical facade, Rev. Strutt was utterly terrified.

To my surprise, when I mentioned this revelation to my mother, she agreed right away.

"Of course he's afraid," she said. "His life is falling apart. We all see it. When I meet up with folks from church, it's all anyone talks about. We all wish there was something we could do."

Emboldened by her openness, I said, "Well, maybe there is. Have you asked him if he needs help?"

"Just come right out and ask?" She side-eyed me from the driver's seat. "That would be a little tacky, don't you think? The poor man's flailing already, wouldn't want to make him feel worse by letting him know we know."

The next day, Monday, Amelia fell while getting up from her desk when the bell rang at the end of Mrs. Lagrange's class. Nobody saw her fall—by that time, everyone in school had tacitly agreed it would be rude to watch Amelia get up and leave a room, or walk down a hall, or travel from place to place in any way. We couldn't treat her like any ordinary person who had to move through space to get from Point A to Point B. She was Amelia, after all.

At the beginning of class, we'd sit at our desks, hers standing empty like a robbed grave, and close our eyes until we heard Amelia's slow, steady steps cross the room; the quiet creaking of her desk as she sat; the shuffling of papers in her backpack. Then, we'd open our eyes, and it would be as if she'd appeared out of thin air. At the end of class, we'd close our eyes again until her steps had faded into the hallway outside.

That day, though, instead of the sound of Amelia rising and leaving, there was a heavy shifting of the desk—metal legs scraping tile, a swish of cloth, and a scrabbling of hands against wood. The thump of a falling body. Stillness.

Nobody moved.

The only sound was a faint, rustling slide of trapped air. Breath haunting the space behind the mask.

I couldn't help but peek. I glanced around the room. Everyone else still had their eyes shut, locked in courteous oblivion. Amelia lay between the front row of desks and the blackboard, her arms feebly circling as if she were trying to swim across the floor.

It had been weeks since I'd dared to look closely at her, and I was shocked at how thin her limbs were, how slow and clumsy her movements. *How long since she's eaten?* Beneath the red elastic, her hair was coarse and matted. Near the edge of the mask, where it traced the side of her face and along her jaw, was a garden of scabs and rashes. Raw red lines showed where the wooden edge had gouged flesh.

I rose from my desk. My heavy steps echoed like distant thunder in the silence as I approached the blackboard, where Mrs. Lagrange had scrawled a line of symbols under the words *PYTHAGOREAN IDENTITY*. Turning my back to the board, I looked down at the fallen queen.

Her motions stilled. The mask tilted up from the floor.

Behind the white eyes, through the dark holes, I saw nothing. I offered my hand.

Amelia's fingers were like twigs wrapped in paper. As I helped her stand, I gripped her forearm, and a hiss of pain reverberated behind the no-mouth. Releasing my grip, I saw bruises bloom where my hand had been. Her flesh had become delicate, vulnerable as a dream.

She stood before me.

I looked again into the holes of the mask's eyes. In the dark, narrow space where Amelia lived, her true eyes burned like newborn stars. No weakness in that burning, no fear. Pain, yes, and anger, and hatred deeper than any ocean. But not a glimmer of fear.

The mask turned away. Picking up her backpack, Amelia stumbled and almost fell again, steadying herself on her desk.

I reached for her on instinct but drew back, thinking of the bruises I'd already inflicted.

"Can you make it?" I said. "Are you all right?"

Her breath rasped against the wood. She fished a notecard from a pocket of her backpack. It was chilly, almost December, but she wore no jacket—I suppose by that point she didn't feel heat or cold. Again, she scrawled a note in ballpoint pen, folded it, handed it to me.

As she left the room, passing slowly between her silent, unseeing classmates like a goddess among her idols, I unfolded the card. *ISAIAH 49:26.*

At lunch, none of the others would talk to me. I don't know what rumors they'd heard, what strange and awful versions of what had happened in Mrs. Lagrange's precalculus class. When I asked Thomas for his Bible, he passed it to me without a word.

Book of Isaiah, chapter 49, verse 26: *And I will feed them that oppress thee with their own flesh; and they shall be drunken with their own blood, as with sweet wine.*

⁂

After school, I found the Strutts' address in the church directory. Biking to their house, I dismounted in the driveway and gazed up at the second floor. Behind the window, two white circles, a delicate nose, a smooth expanse. Behind the mask, a face I didn't dare remember, a face I wished I could see.

The doorbell played a tinny hymn. From inside, I heard shouts, a body blundering against furniture. When Rev. Strutt opened the door, his shirt was half-tucked and his hair uncombed. He swayed in the doorway, his breath gin-sour, his eyes burning like embers.

"What the fuck do you want?" he said.

"I'd like to talk to Amelia," I said.

He laughed, coughed, laughed again. "Be my guest." He stepped back, sweeping his arm in a mockery of welcome.

When I hesitated, he beckoned, snarling. "Are you going to fucking come in or not?"

I stepped across the threshold. The house smelled like sweat, trash, rot, the decayed wreckage of a home. From the entrance hall, I could see a living room full of overturned furniture, empty liquor bottles, and dirty plates teetering precariously on every surface. Finally my eyes landed on a stairway leading to the darkened second floor.

"About time someone came to see that girl," Rev. Strutt muttered, closing the door. "Fine bunch of people you are. Fine group of friends. No one for months. Orphan girl, all alone."

I looked away from him, embarrassed. I wasn't sure what I'd expected, but it hadn't been this.

"Well, she's not totally alone," I said. "She's got you."

"Ha!" He slapped his hand against the wall, hard. If it hurt, he was too drunk to feel it. "Me! And who comes to see *me*? No one. Widowed husband. Grieving. Lost my world, lost everything. These fucking people come to hear me read them the fucking Bible on Sundays and won't see me, won't help me! Leaving me alone with that girl, that—" He slapped the wall again.

Enough of this shit, I thought. I turned toward the stairway. "Amelia?" I called. "Are you up there?"

"She's up there, all right," Rev. Strutt said. "Always. I stay down here, she stays up there. Does she come down, help her poor father? Clean up a little, help around the house? No, nothing!"

"Listen, I'm not here for this. I'm here for Amelia. Did you ever think about the help she needs? When's the last time she ate?"

"She doesn't." He strode past me, and I followed him up the stairs. "Ever since she put on that goddamn mask. Too good to help her father. And now you're here for her. Who's coming for *me*?"

The hallway upstairs was pitch-black. I flipped the lightswitch, but no lights came on. Rev. Strutt hammered on a door, screaming in the dark.

"Amelia! You open this fucking door right fucking now!"

The weak light of late November spilled into the hallway as she opened the door. Amelia stood silhouetted in the feeble glow, her emaciated body seeming to float in the heavy, stuffy air of the house.

"About fucking time," Rev. Strutt said.

Amelia lifted a finger to the mask, pressed it against the empty space beneath the delicate nose. Then, quick as a wish, she thrust her hand into her father's face. The twigs of her fingers scratched at his lips, pried his mouth open, squirmed into the void behind his incredulous snarl. The hallway echoed with a muffled shout, then a gargling yelp as a cord of muscle leapt on Amelia's arm, her arm thin and wasted but strong, strong. She pulled her hand back with a sodden rip. From her clenched fingers dangled a dripping rag of flesh, a puny, conquered banner.

In the dimness, the liquid pouring from Rev. Strutt's lips was black as ink. He fell to his knees, clapped his hands over his mouth, bowed his head. Kneeling in the dark hallway, humbled before the mask, he looked like a figure out of legend, a courteous knight paying obeisance to his lady.

The mask swung toward me. Just enough light fell through the doorway to show the birch-bark circles. The fiery points that shone from behind them needed no sun. I stared into the radiance of a sovereignty bought at the price of absolute alienation. Amelia's gleaming eyes gazed back at me from a distance beyond endurance, a solitude past understanding.

I took a step toward her, quivering with terror and amazement. When her gaze didn't obliterate me, I took another. Soon I was at the doorway. Beside me, Rev. Strutt knelt in a pool of blood, his tongueless moans growing weaker.

He'd received the due punishment for his discourtesy. I strove to deserve better.

I raised my hands, pressing my fingers lightly to the sides of the mask. The wood was smooth and cool.

"May I?" I asked.

Ever so slightly, Amelia inclined her head.

As I lifted the mouthless veil, the squelch and stench of purulent flesh turned the hallway to a bower of corpse flowers, but I maintained my composure. I would be a courteous servant.

Freed from the gentle curve of the mask, Amelia's barbed maw glistened hungrily in the dying light. But I didn't flinch. I would be a courteous servant.

Her eyes blazed brighter, twin furnaces of devouring splendor. I returned their gaze, unblinking. I would be a courteous servant.

The shining eyes flickered down to Amelia's collapsed father, back up to me. Understanding, I nodded, found my way through the dark hallway and to the stairs. Behind me, I heard the rustling squish as Amelia knelt on the blood-soaked carpet, heard the viscid rending of flesh torn from bone, the chewing and swallowing, the moans of satisfaction after long hunger. I heard it all, but I kept silent, and I never turned to look. It's impolite to watch your queen eat.

Winter Savory

Before I went away to college, my parents and I always spent Christmas with my father's relatives in New Mexico, and even with the obliviousness of youth, I could tell my mother hated every minute of it. When I'd show her the shiny new presents I'd just unwrapped, she'd smile and murmur her approval, but her eyes were dull and evasive. While the rest of us sang about Rudolph and jolly old St. Nick, she'd sit silent, her gaze wandering to the living room windows and the darkness beyond.

At the time, I thought she just didn't get along with her in-laws. How could I have guessed the anguish of her situation, the torture of knowing that her family was celebrating the true holiday without her? Out of concern for me—for my innocence—she endured that agony for seventeen years, until I was finally ready to experience a real Christmas.

When I heard about the change to our usual holiday routine, I thought it was a simple matter of convenience. I was finishing up my first semester at SMU, and my mother's parents lived not too far from Dallas, out in the country to the northwest of Fort Worth. My parents and I planned to rendezvous there on

Christmas Eve, spend a few days with the extended family, then caravan home to Amarillo for the rest of my winter break.

I drove up on the afternoon of the twenty-fourth, under a sky swarmed with low, creeping clouds. As soon as my grandparents' house came into view, a distant blot against fields of yellow-gray stubble, an uneasy tingling began to spread through my chest. Something about the place felt wrong. Was it only that I was driving from the south, where before, on our July visits, we'd always come down from the north, so that now the house seemed turned around backward, showing me the wrong face? No, it became clear as I approached that the house itself was different. Windows I remembered as friendly and inviting were now hollow and cavernous. The roof looked steeper, the walls taller, everything crooked and precarious. My unease grew stronger, the tingling rising to my face and flowing through my limbs.

Driving closer, I realized what made the difference. It was the trees, the stand of ash and elm and oak that surrounded the property. In summer, their leaves wove a flickering shroud that made the house seem a roadside shrine, lapped in unearthly green fire. Now, the trees stood bare, bending their naked boughs over the dead grass like catacomb arches, all the trunks' knots and holes exposed and glaring balefully from the dark wood. In the midst of this skeletal throng, the house looked cowed and humbled, begging for mercy.

My grandparents' driveway was already crowded with cars. As I walked to the front door with a stack of presents balanced in my arms, the trees shook accusing branches at me. Anxiety festered in my stomach. Wondering how many of the gathered relatives would recognize or remember me, I rang the bell with my elbow.

Before the bell finished ringing, the door flew open to reveal my mother's older sister. I hadn't seen Aunt Phoebe in years, but she looked just as I remembered her, red-cheeked and smiling, radiating health and contentment. On her red knit sweater, a deer leapt in white silhouette. A pair of fuzzy antlers rose from a headband atop her gray curls. Behind her, the entryway glowed warmly, green wreaths hanging on the walls. I began to feel calm, happy, welcome.

"Look at you!" Aunt Phoebe brushed her hands over my shoulders. "All grown up and ready to party. Let me get those." Before I could protest, she snatched the presents from my arms.

I followed her into the house. Entering the living room, she shouted, "Attention, everyone! Little Daniel has joined us!" I smiled and blushed. As the youngest among the grandchildren, I'd always be "Little Daniel," no matter my age.

The living room was full of relatives, aunts and uncles and cousins lounging on couches along the holly-hung walls. Opposite the doorway, ensconced between the television and a huge tree dripping with glass icicles, my grandmother sat in her rocking chair, a green blanket tucked around her legs. Everyone wore the same sweater as Aunt Phoebe, the same white shadow rampant on the same red field. Fuzzy antlers crowned every head.

"I feel ... underdressed," I said. "Did I miss an email?"

Aunt Phoebe laughed. "Not at all. As a matter of fact, we've got a whole getup waiting for you upstairs, deer and antlers and all. Only if you want to play along, of course. It's just a little fun we like to have, this time of year." She carried my presents toward the tree, where a huge pile of colored packages had already accumulated.

I exchanged greetings with the rest of the family. Some I'd seen fairly recently, others not since I was a small child, but it didn't seem to make a difference; everyone was equally friendly, equally delighted to see me. My uncles shook my hand and thumped my shoulder. My aunts gave me quick, tight hugs, darting in and away like hummingbirds. My cousins grinned and winked and asked how I liked it at college. My grandmother motioned me down to give me a peck on the cheek. The only people missing were my parents, due to arrive later that evening, and my grandfather, whose recliner sat empty across from the television, draped with a pale blue quilt.

"Where's Grandpa?" I asked my grandmother.

"He's in bed, sleeping off an upset stomach. My stew didn't agree with him."

"You made stew?"

"It may surprise you to learn that there's more than one person in this house who knows how to use a stove!"

It did surprise me. I'd never known my grandmother to cook much of anything. When I'd visited, my grandfather had always been the cook, and his stew was my favorite, thick and dark, big chunks of meat bobbing in a swirl of herbs and vegetables fresh from his garden.

"Now listen," my grandmother said, folding her thin hands on her green-blanketed lap. "When your grandpa makes stew, he puts summer savory in it. Ugh!" She wrinkled her nose and bared her teeth in disgust. "It turns my stomach. So weak and flavorless. Cowardly. Me, I use winter savory. Something you can really taste."

For the first time since entering the house, I felt a twinge of the unease I'd experienced outside. I'd never heard my grandmother say a word against my grandfather's cooking, and I'd never seen her face take on an expression like that, repulsed and triumphant, the kind of look an empress might give a criminal on his way to the scaffold. I shifted uneasily. "I always liked Grandpa's stew."

My grandmother's face softened. "Well, just wait till you try mine." She looked over my shoulder and shouted, "Corey!"

My mother's younger brother stood up from a couch, antlers wobbling above his thinning red hair. "What is it, Mom?"

"Heat up a bowl of stew for Little Daniel here."

"Oh, I'm fine," I said. "I had lunch before I started out."

"Just a little taste. Come on, Corey, hustle!"

Uncle Corey brought me a bowl of what looked like the stew I remembered, though at that season, I supposed, the vegetables must have been store-bought. I raised a spoonful to my lips. It was certainly richer than my grandfather's stew, spicier, with a citrus tang and an earthy, almost metallic undertone that lingered on my tongue.

"Now isn't it sad that your grandpa's stomach can't handle something like that, something with real flavor?" My grandmother made a sound deep in her throat, half-chuckle, half-growl. "What a pathetic weakling."

Startled, I glanced around the room, but no one else seemed to have heard. I'd never known either of my mother's parents to say anything like that about anybody, let alone one another. I'd always seen them as the sweetest, most devoted old couple in the world. I thought of the changed house, the stripped and reaching trees, the desolate shell surrounding the living room's kernel of warmth and love. Something beyond anxiety slithered around my heart, something like terror.

From across the room, Aunt Phoebe called out, "Mom, quit hogging Little Daniel! Give the rest of us a chance to pick up some of that college wisdom." Her voice, friendly and cheerful as ever, soothed my worries, my half-suspicions. Maybe I'd just caught my grandmother at a grouchy moment. Maybe she felt guilty because her stew had made my grandfather sick, and she was taking her worries out on him in his absence. Looking down at her in her rocking chair, I saw a kind old woman smiling up at me, her eyes bright with holiday mirth. I returned her smile and went to circulate among the family.

I spent the afternoon in the living room with my aunts and uncles and cousins, chatting and laughing, telling jokes and stories. Every so often, a family member would leave for a few minutes and return with some new bit of decoration, a chain of dried leaves or a pair of twisted branches joined to make antlers. These knickknacks collected around the room, gradually covering the end tables and filling the corners. Warm talk flowed in the air. A scene of utmost harmony and affection, with one strange detail: as the relatives moved around the room, they always avoided the space around my grandfather's recliner, his blue quilt ostracized among the red sweaters, the phantom deer. I wondered if the chair gave off some foul odor I couldn't detect.

When the light in the windows had faded to a dull blue-gray, my grandmother cleared her throat and rose from her chair, rubbing her hands together.

"All right!" she said. "I've listened to your bellies grumbling long enough. Children, come help me in the kitchen."

She strode from the room, my mother's sisters and brothers trailing behind her. The spouses and grandchildren grinned after the antlered procession. Uncle Corey's husband turned to me, rubbing his belly. "Won't be long now. Just wait till you get a taste," he said.

We sat in near silence. Expectation floated in the room like smoke, so palpable that my stomach tingled with renewed anxiety. Through the windows, I watched the trees' bare limbs shake and gesture in the wind. The trees no longer menaced but beckoned, summoning me out of the stifling house and into the fresh, cold evening. I rose and hurried to the door.

"Lost your appetite?" Uncle Corey's husband called after me.

"Just grabbing my bag out of the car before it gets dark," I said.

Outside, the wind made alien music in the branches, a chorus of whistles and rattles. Low clouds scurried overhead. All nature was in motion, churning around my grandparents' house like the tides around an ancient, upthrusting rock. In the few hours since I'd arrived, some obscure balance had shifted; now it was the house that vaunted and dominated, the trees that cowered and quailed. The house seemed a shrine again, but now a shrine of death, holding the wintry world in thrall. The naked trees quaked in the wind, miserable worshipers pleading for intercession.

Light from the windows behind me painted long yellow strokes across the dead grass, gleaming reflected in my car's windshield at the end of the driveway. *I could leave,* I thought. *Drive straight to Amarillo and wait for my parents there. Powers are working here, vast and dreadful. I could just leave.*

I didn't leave. I'm a nervous person, but no coward. I went to my car, got my bag, returned to the house. When I opened the door, a flood of delicious smells washed over me, and I knew I'd made the right choice.

My bedroom was on the second floor. Visiting in summer, I'd always slept on a couch in the living room, but this time I'd been given a room all my own, with a queen-sized bed and a window looking down on the backyard.

A glance through the window showed a square of dirt strewn with dead leaves and stalks, set in the withered grass like an ashen jewel—the broken wreckage of my grandfather's garden. I'd seen the garden only in its green vigor, a profusion of stems and leaves laid out so densely yet so carefully it could have been its own self-contained cosmos, rows of vegetables and herbs arranged as intricately as a labyrinth. All ruined now.

On the bed, I found the sweater Aunt Phoebe had promised spread out on the blanket, the antlered headgear lying on the pillow.

"Dinner's ready!" Uncle Corey called up from below.

I hesitated beside the bed, waves of feeling rolling over me—first a raw surge of anxiety, then sheer terror, as if I were sliding toward the edge of a bottomless pit. Finally, an intense, almost manic curiosity seized me. Something was about to happen, something strange and terrible, and I wanted to know what. I put on the sweater and antlers and went down to dinner, the headband tight around my skull.

In the dining room, the family sat around a long table covered with food: piles of rolls, heaps of yams and carrots, a giant pot of black-eyed peas, a green salad with sliced vegetables shining like coins among the curly-edged leaves, silky mashed potatoes with gravy as thick and golden as honey. In the center of everything, slices of roast meat lay in a huge round platter, tiny droplets of clear sauce quivering on the reddish-brown flesh. A dozen odors rolled and coiled in the air, swirls of otherworldly incense that made my head swim.

The chairs at the head and foot of the table were empty. Aunt Phoebe sat at the left hand of the head, opposite another empty chair. Beaming genially at me, she pointed at the seat across from her. I took my place.

"Now we're just waiting for Mom and Dad," Aunt Phoebe said. She ran her eyes along the laden table, licking her lips.

No one else spoke. Silence reigned, the total silence of all-consuming anticipation.

At last, footsteps came from the back of the house, two people walking in slow lockstep. All eyes turned to the open door, the dim hallway beyond. The footsteps drew closer and closer, keeping their dignified cadence. Hunger and curiosity and dread whirled and tangled in me, a silent, frozen frenzy. When my grandparents appeared in the doorway, I bit my lip to keep from crying out.

My grandmother stood behind the empty chair to my left, motionless as a queen in marble, while my grandfather made his solitary way along the table. I'd seen him a few months earlier, visiting in July with my parents as usual, but he seemed to have aged ten years since then. His face was sunken, all wrinkles and dangling jowls, a few gray strands straggling across his mottled scalp. As he passed behind Aunt Phoebe, the folds of his thin, pale-blue bathrobe fell open to reveal a mass of creased, flabby flesh, studded with black moles and knots of bushy hair. His gait was halfway between a shuffle and a limp, as if one of his legs had withered and the other was broken.

Noticing my distress, Aunt Phoebe looked me in the eyes, smiled warmly and winked. "It's okay," she stage-whispered. "This is how it goes."

At last, my grandfather reached the foot of the table. Stooped and panting, he stood behind the empty chair. He seemed to be waiting for my grandmother to make the first move, giving her a look of impatience that became a glare of furious loathing. She remained standing for what felt like hours before a tiny smile of triumph curled her lips and she sat. My grandfather collapsed into his chair with a groan.

My grandmother clasped her hands over her plate. "Good food, good meat, good God, let's eat."

The meal was the most delicious I'd ever had, everything cooked and seasoned to perfection, every dish perfectly balanced against every other. My tongue glowed with spices and seasonings I'd never tasted before.

"Grandma, where did you find all these ingredients in the middle of winter?" I asked.

She arched her eyebrows. "I have my sources."

"It's too bad Mom and Dad aren't here for this," I said.

"There'll be plenty left over when they get here," Aunt Phoebe said. "And anyway, it's your first Christmas dinner with the family. Better if your parents aren't here."

I wasn't sure what she meant by that, but I soon learned. As the dishes circulated and the odors wafted around the table, the conversation grew raucous, lewd, shocking. It became a kind of competition, everyone vying to tell the most outrageous story, the most uninhibited confession. My aunts and uncles shared intimate details that left me reeling. My cousins related appalling exploits, tales of carnal adventure I never would have believed if the atmosphere around that table had permitted anything less than utter honesty. The room throbbed with talk of fluids, holes, protrusions, cravings suffered and satisfied, all conceivable comminglings. Applause broke out when one of my uncles described what he'd done to his neighbor's cat, and again when two cousins detailed what they'd done to each other. My grandmother chewed silently all the while, a sly twinkle in her eye.

"Little Daniel's awfully quiet," Uncle Corey said, grinning at me from the seat next to my grandfather.

Ashamed of my inexperience, I shook my head. "Not much worth telling, sad to say."

"Come on, Little Daniel," Aunt Phoebe said. "We all know what you college types get up to. Spill!"

Uncle Corey clinked a fork against his plate. "Daniel! Daniel!" he chanted.

My cousins took up the rhythm, drumming the table with their fists. "Daniel! Daniel!"

Blushing, I ventured a story or two. My clumsy dorm-room explorations paled in comparison to what had gone before, but my contributions were well-received, cousins hooting and aunts shrieking and uncles grunting appreciatively. As the feast continued and tale after tale followed, we seemed to talk and laugh and howl for hours in a whirl of frenzied abandon. Only my grandfather remained outside the magic circle, scowling and picking at his plate. While the rest of us crammed ourselves full of good things, he took only a few small mouthfuls, his face twisted as if tasting some bitter medicine.

Finally sated, we sprawled in our chairs, sighing dreamily. My grandmother leaned forward on her elbows and fixed my grandfather with a glittering basilisk stare.

"What did you think of dinner, sweetheart?" she said, her voice thick with derision.

Silence filled the room. My grandfather pursed his lips, spat out a single word. "Filth."

My grandmother rose. With slow and stately steps, she stalked to the foot of the table. For a moment she stood beside my grandfather's chair, looking at him with something like pity. Then, she raised her hand and struck him hard across the face. Flecks of spittle arced from his lips.

I was too stunned to do anything but stare open-mouthed as my grandmother returned to the head of the table and resumed her seat. The others all sat quiet and still. I looked at Aunt Phoebe, who gave me another warm smile, another wink.

"This is how it goes," she whispered. "Watch."

She stood, crossed the room to where her father sat, and hit him again. His head snapped back, jowls trembling. Aunt Phoebe went back to her place.

One by one, the others rose and struck, the slap of their hands against dry, withered flesh piercing the silence like the beat of a funeral drum. Red droplets rolled from my grandfather's nostrils and the corners of his mouth. He leaned forward once to dribble blood onto his dinner plate, but otherwise he sat passive, unresisting. Only his eyes seemed fully alive, blazing ferociously along the table at my grandmother, who answered his glare with a gaze of imperious satisfaction.

When everyone but me had taken their turn, Aunt Phoebe stood and came around to my side. She leaned over to murmur in my ear, "You don't have to hit him hard if you don't want to."

In a daze, I staggered toward the foot of the table. The family waited with bated breath to see what I would do. Slowly approaching my grandfather, I pondered my options. A light smack, a token tap ... or should I bolt from the room, refuse to play along? Surely he's suffered enough, I thought, but as I looked down at the old man—so weak and powerless, so utterly without defense—I felt my pity curdle to disgust. How dare this decrepit husk pollute our revel? I slapped his face with all my strength.

His head crumpled aside and dangled over his shoulder as if he'd lost consciousness, but I saw his open eyes still smoldering, still fixed on my grandmother.

I stood paralyzed with shame and terror. My palm stung from the slap, and the sting seemed to travel up my arm like an infection, a guilty curse. But when the sting reached my heart, I realized that what had entered my hand was not poison but power, power that had been stolen, usurped, now flowing back to its right place.

Slumped beneath me, my grandfather looked even weaker than he had a moment ago, even more contemptible. Bloody drool trickled over his lips.

Torn between compassion and revulsion, I wrenched myself away and went back to my seat. Across the table, Aunt Phoebe gave me a thumbs-up. "You did good," she whispered.

An electronic tone sang out through the silent house. Uncle Corey hurried to answer the door. A few moments later, he returned with my parents, and an uproar filled the room as everyone rose to greet the final arrivals. I saw my mother's eyes shining, radiant with joy. After the hugs and greetings, she crossed the room to her father's collapsed form and gave him a gentle slap, almost a pat.

With dinner finished, the family returned to the living room, where the rest of the evening passed in a blur of talk and laughter. Around midnight, I realized I could barely keep my eyes open. I said goodnight and stumbled toward bed. On my way to the stairs, I glanced into the dining room and saw my grandfather still slumped at the foot of the table, his pale chest gleaming between his robe's blue folds.

A raging thirst woke me in the middle of the night. Tiptoeing downstairs to the kitchen, I found my mother sipping a cup of tea. She pointed to a second cup sitting on the counter. I took a sip—honey-golden, mild, soothing.

"Mom," I said, fragrant steam wreathing my face, "what's happening?"

She shrugged. "It's Christmas."

"Okay, but ... what's happening?"

She swallowed the last of her tea, set the cup down with a sigh. "It's winter. The deepest depth of winter. Death is creeping all around, draining the life from the grass, the trees. Trying to get inside the house. It takes a strong hand to hold the door closed against death. If the hand on the door proves weak, another hand will strike it down. What do you call it when one hand strikes the other?"

I shook my head. "I don't know."

My mother smiled. "A revolution."

I turned to the window above the sink. Thick flakes were falling, glimmering between darkness and darkness as they passed through the light from the kitchen. "Are we coming back for our visit next July?" I asked.

"Sure we are. If you want, we can even come back in June."

"What happens in June?"

"What do you think revolution means, Daniel? It means turning around, and around, and around. The year is a wheel. Every hand has its season." She patted me on the shoulder. "I know this is confusing. I was confused too, my first real Christmas. But you're in college now. It's time you learned these things."

A hot blush spread across my face. I went back to bed.

I woke to the sight of Aunt Phoebe's antlered head leaning through my half-open door. "Cock-a-doodle-doo, sleepyhead! Rise and shine. Presents in thirty minutes."

I showered, dressed, put on my red sweater and fuzzy antlers. Outside, a bright skin of snow lay on the world. My grandfather's garden had become a ravaged palace, snow-whitened stalks lying like fallen pillars. The sky was the pale blue of my grandfather's bathrobe.

Uncle Corey met me at the bottom of the stairs with a cup of black coffee. "Just in time," he said. "Everybody's ready. Now, when you go in there, just remember, it's okay. This is how it goes."

Sipping my coffee, I followed Uncle Corey to the living room. Again, my aunts and uncles and cousins crowded the couches, now joined by my parents. My father smiled blandly, gave me a good-morning wave. At the far end of the room, between the television and the tree, lay a spectacle that froze my blood with holy dread. I stood transfixed, my mouth open, staring.

Enthroned in her rocking chair, my grandmother sat shrouded in a red robe patterned with white swords, a wreath of vines resting in her lap. From her head rose a crown of branches carved and bent into antlers, dripping red berries and gobbets of meat impaled on the sharpened points. Her face was absolutely expressionless, as blank and regal as a Paleolithic idol.

Across from the television, on his recliner, my grandfather lay naked except for a pale wrapping around his loins. At first, I thought he was wearing a diaper, but a second glance revealed a thick, whitish-yellow serpent twined around his waist and between his legs, its coils shifting and flexing, its diamond-shaped head resting on his crotch. Green vines bound his forehead, wrists, and ankles—poison ivy, judging from the rashes that splotched his skin. The snake blinked its black eyes at me, flickered its red tongue.

My grandmother gestured at the couch where my parents sat. "Join us," she said. I squeezed in between my mother and father, clutching my cup of coffee, my shaking hand making the black liquid dance.

I turned toward my father, tried to ask what he made of all this, but the words stuck in my throat. Still, he must have read the question in my eyes. He shrugged. "When in Rome ..."

The rocking chair creaked as my grandmother leaned forward. "Phoebe," she said. "Distribute the blessings."

Aunt Phoebe went to the tree and took a package from the pile. Examining the label, she grinned. "It's for Little Daniel." She approached me and laid the present at my feet. "Don't open it yet," she whispered.

Phoebe handed out the presents one by one, until the huge pile was exhausted.

"Reveal the blessings," my grandmother said.

We all opened our presents, everyone except my grandfather, immobilized on his recliner. There was the usual tearing and crumpling of paper, the ritual exclamations and thanks. My presents were mostly what I'd expected, books, clothes, gift cards. Uncle Corey had given me a box of condoms; I blushed and hid it under a pair of jeans.

The unwrapping done, my grandmother cleared her throat. "Phoebe," she said.

"Yes, my queen?"

"Let us play a game."

Small, secret smiles lit up the faces around me.

"What game would you like to play, my queen?" Phoebe said.

My grandmother grinned at my bound, helpless grandfather. "Let us play Whip the King."

Phoebe nodded, her cheeks flushed with excitement. "As you desire."

Reaching into the folds of her robe, my grandmother drew out a greenish-brown bundle tied with red string. It was a sheaf of foot-long stems, woody shafts bristling with dried, yellow-green leaves. Phoebe carried the bundle around the room, handing us each a stem. The leaves gave off a rich, spicy smell that filled the air.

"All rise," my grandmother said.

Somehow, without being told, I knew what was expected of me, of all of us. I knew how it would go.

"Approach the king."

We formed a ring around my grandfather's recliner. His eyes rolled furiously in their sockets, white foam bubbling from the corners of his mouth. The serpent at his waist flexed and writhed.

"Whip!" my grandmother shouted.

We raised our stems of winter savory and brought them down sharply on my grandfather's body, raised them again and brought them down again. Red welts scored his flesh, white ichor streamed from burst blisters where the vines chafed.

As I lashed my grandfather, his skin opening like wrapping paper under my scourge, I knew in my heart that what I did was right. The King of Summer had failed to hold life's door firm, failed again as he always had and always would. The price of failure was shame, and suffering, and ridicule. Only the Queen of Winter could keep death at bay. Snarling with fury, I whipped and whipped again.

"Enough," my grandmother said, rising. We dropped our stems and stepped back. My grandfather lay bleeding and quivering, his pale flesh scribbled over with seeping red strokes.

Standing at the foot of the recliner, my grandmother held out her hand. The serpent uncoiled itself from my grandfather, curled around her arm and nestled its head in her palm. Under the snake, my grandfather was naked, shriveled.

My grandmother raised her hand to her face, opened her lips wide. Her eyes rolled back with pleasure as the snake's head slid from her palm into her mouth. Then, growling deep in her throat, she brought her teeth together with a sharp click. Blood fountained from the severed flesh, reddening my grandmother's lips, spattering us all as the snake's headless body flailed and spasmed.

My grandfather groaned and twitched. He curled on the recliner like a fetus. My grandmother threw the bloody snake onto his shivering body and spat the head into his face.

"Clean him up," she said. She returned to her rocking chair, blood flowing down her chin.

We washed my grandfather's wounds and carried him to bed, where he stayed for the next few days while the rest of us celebrated the Queen of Winter's new reign. My mother seemed happier than I'd ever seen her. Truly, it must have been torture for her to miss so many real Christmases, to sit far away and wonder how the year's wheel was turning.

As my parents and I were loading up our cars for the drive home, my grandfather emerged onto the porch. He tottered weakly between Aunt Phoebe and Uncle Corey, his arms flung across their shoulders. Around the house, in the bright, still morning, the naked trees stood motionless. Death had been appeased.

Uncle Corey shook my hand, wished me luck in my spring classes. Aunt Phoebe gave me a crushing hug. I turned to face my grandfather.

He was no king now, not even a deposed one, only a beaten old man. His face was puffy and bruised, his forehead lumpy with sagging blisters. Still, he looked healthier than before. Younger, even. His blue eyes sparkled.

I didn't dare touch him. I leaned close and whispered, "Sorry, Grandpa."

He chuckled. "Sorry for what? That's how it goes. And anyway," he said with a wink, "I'll get her back come June. I always do."

Osculum

Swaying on the dance floor, bathed in red light, Julian leans forward, and quick as the thought takes shape in Kathy's mind—*finally, finally*—his lips are on hers, pressing at first very lightly as if against a rotted-out wall ready to crumble at the slightest touch, then more firmly, gradually more firmly as his face moves closer, his lips' aperture opening, and she returns the pressure, answers the increase, so that his lips deform under the impulse of hers and hers under his, closeness pushing their mouths open, *finally, finally*, her tongue moving across his lips, his teeth, his tongue pushing against hers, his teeth hard against her lips, bony, unsheathed, harder and harder, she grips the back of his head, his hair curling between her fingers, she pulls him forward, his hands on her face, palms riding a thin tide of sweat across her cheeks to the sides of her head, each bringing the other closer, pulling the other in, teeth hard against teeth as if no lips interposed, and now is when she first tastes blood, the dark tang of it sliding between their tongues so that she doesn't know if it's her blood or his, now he first starts to make a sound, a whining sound like a dog smelling a stranger, now she feels new wetness and a sting in her lips as the teeth begin to press through, hard edges into red flesh, her own teeth entering her lips from behind as a cloud of red liquid light fills her mouth and she pulls him closer and he pulls her closer, pain rushing and roaring in her mouth, teeth pressing directly on teeth as her fingers clutch his head so tight her nails dig into his scalp, his hands squeezing her head as if seeking to meet in the middle of her brain, hands pulling heads ever closer, further, and her eyes that have been squeezed shut now open and flow, two hot cataracts gushing down her cheeks as her eyes roll in ecstatic terror, *what's happening, why are we doing this,* she sees his open eyes flashing, reflecting red light, more radiant with fear than with light, she hears herself making noises, sounding like a crushed animal, panic explodes from his weeping, bloodshot eyes, panic piercing her own eyes to thunder and echo in her brain, *please, please, please, please,* her eyes rolling, frantic, the room flashing red around her, the dance floor crammed with bodies pressed together, red-lit fountains pouring from heads mashed against heads, hands tangled around hands like lumps of crumpled wire as her hands now crumple, her fingers snap and fold, not feeling like fingers anymore, drooping and twisting, his fingers popping like firecrackers behind her ears, what were hands now jagged shards wrapped in meat, the meat always there, hidden, now exposed, inescapable, horror and pain and wild delight swirling in her brain like the hot blood and meat that swirl in her mouth as her teeth shatter and his mouth enters hers, the stumps and spears of his wrecked teeth raking her gums, her burst, streaming tongue flapping against the crushed pulp that was his lips, flapping like a burning flag as their faces begin to collapse, noses and chins buckling under the unbearable, ever more unbearable pressure, blood pouring from all over, their faces two torn, flowing masses, one mass, one flesh, and the thought howls in her mind as their voices are howling, gurgling howls through gags of meat and blood, bubbling in springs of blood, *love is union, love is union*, red light falling on red blood falling on red flesh falling into itself, falling into absolute union, selfsame, red and red and red and red and red.

Graceful Degradation

The nurse wears my dead father's face as he smiles down on my bound, quaking body and says in the voice of Ned Flanders, "Just try to relax. The doctor's on her way."

He wipes a cool, damp cloth across my burning forehead. I try to say, "Thank you," but the loop locks me in, and I scream what I've been screaming since I crawled into the hospital this morning. "GET THIS FUCKING THING OUT OF ME!"

The nurse takes a step back. His head flies apart into a cloud of fragments that swoop and swirl like starlings in murmuration before reforming into a face I've seen in a hundred puff pieces on the news, a hundred ads on the subway. *It's a Whole New Way to THINK!*

I never noticed the resemblance to my father before. Now that I've seen it, it's undeniable.

"I'll go check on the doctor," the nurse says. His nasal voice squeals and buzzes, the pattern matcher searching for a closer fit, then settles back into Ned as he says, again, "Just try to relax."

Another scream is gathering in my chest. Desperate to break out of the loop, I tighten every muscle in my body, strain my wrists and ankles against the Kevlar straps holding me to the bed. Hours of involuntary shrieks and howls have turned my throat to a raw, throbbing clot of ragged meat. If I scream again, I don't think I'll ever stop.

Behind my eyes, the loop's knot loosens. No scream. I unclench my body with a relieved sigh.

The sigh sends another runaway process spiraling through my brain, and I start laughing hysterically. Not better.

The door closes with a sound like metal tearing through metal. The nurse is gone. Just like my parents, just like the man from the subway ads, just like my miracle cure, just like my mind. All gone.

Nothing to do but wait for the doctor. I close my eyes and listen to the laughter flooding out of me, thinking of another laugh in another hospital room.

———

The man on the video call looked so much like his publicity photos, the same slicked-down hair and dazzling eyes and glittering smile, that I couldn't help but giggle.

"I'm sorry," I mumbled, straightening the half of my face that could move. "It's just such a surprise. And you look exactly like you do on the news."

The smile widened, glittered brighter. "Well, that's what I pay my people for."

The lawyer sitting in the corner of the room cleared her throat, leaned forward in the plastic chair. "If I could ask us to move things along, please," she said. "We have quite a few of these meetings scheduled for today. Of course, you understand that if ..."

"He understands," the man on the screen said, no longer smiling. All business. "He understands perfectly. I can tell."

I understood a few things, at least. I understood that I was lying in a hospital bed with a broken skull and a traumatized frontal lobe. I understood that, even in the best-case scenario, it would take months or years of physical therapy before I could stand, let alone walk. In the worst-case scenario, I'd be paralyzed for the rest of my life, not to mention all the other symptoms that might be hiding in the crannies of my damaged brain, waiting to slither forth. Loss of judgment, loss of speech, mood swings, personality changes. Who I'd be in a few months was anybody's guess. I understood that much.

I understood, too, that I was the sole survivor of the wreck that had killed my parents and everyone in the other car. And no matter how many times I told myself it was all the other driver's fault, that he'd swerved out of his lane with no warning, right into the side of us at seventy miles per hour, I also understood that I was lying to myself, that if I'd been paying closer attention I could have done something—slammed on the brakes, pulled over onto the shoulder, anything. It was my fault they were dead. I understood that, all the way down to my shattered bones.

As if he could read my mind, the man on the screen said, "Aside from the physical and cognitive benefits, our trials have shown that over two thirds of ThinkingCap recipients report improvements in mood, in outlook, in self-esteem. It's not just a whole new way to think. It's a whole new way to feel. To feel good about yourself."

I only half-listened to the rest of his well-rehearsed spiel with its rattled-off numbers and heartwarming anecdotes, its dumbed-down explanations of cortical implants and neural networks. I already knew what he was offering me. A second mind inside my mind, one that could learn to do all the things the wreck had made me forget. Maybe even learn to forget the things I feared I'd always remember.

And if it didn't work, if something went terribly wrong ... wouldn't that be what I deserved?

The spiel wound down. The lawyer fidgeted in the corner. The man on the screen smiled wide.

"Any questions?" he said.

"Well ..." I hesitated, straining to recall the details of an article I'd read, one of the few skeptical eddies in a surging tide of admiration.

"Nothing's off-limits. After all, this is your brain we're talking about!"

It flickered at the edge of my memory. Something about monkeys ...

"Monkeys," I mumbled.

"Excuse me?"

Blurting out half-formed thoughts, was that one of the symptoms? Loss of inhibition?

Half of my mouth smiled apologetically. "I'm sorry, I didn't mean to ..."

"It's perfectly all right." If my slip confused or offended him, he didn't show it. His smile was wider than ever. "You must be thinking of that story about our animal trials. That piece of so-called journalism. Let me assure you, it was all wildly exaggerated. Disgruntled ex-employees spreading rumors. Have we encountered setbacks in the course of our research? Of course! That's how science works. I assure you, though, we've always proceeded with the utmost concern for the well-being of our trial subjects. If anything, we might have been a little too careful! The review board was all set to approve us for human trials last year, but I said no, let's not rush. Give it a bit more time, make sure we've ironed out every last kink."

The lawyer stood up, her shoes squeaking on the linoleum floor. "I'm sorry, but we really do have a lot of meetings scheduled. If you've decided to withdraw from the trial ..."

"No," I said. I closed my eyes to think.

A wall of metal surging toward me out of the darkness. My parents' faces twisting in panic.

I opened my eyes. The man on the screen smiled.

———◦———

Tears and spit soak my pillow as I sob with laughter. My teeth gnash uncontrollably, punctuating my guffaws with a morse-code click of bone on bone. I plant my tongue against the roof of my mouth to keep from biting it off.

I stare up at the ceiling, trying to focus my mind—my actual mind, not the thousand counterfeits running wild through the madhouse corridors of my brain. The real me is still somewhere in there, hiding in some corner or crawlspace. It must be.

The holes in the ceiling's acoustical tile start to dance as the pattern matcher seizes them. They shift and melt like clouds, forming a wreath of lilies, a bloom of jellyfish, an off-white sky full of black stars. A tattered face smashed against a headrest.

I squeeze my eyes shut, so tight that the processor skips a cycle and I stop laughing. My mouth hangs open, my tongue lolls. A moment's peace.

It can't last. Soon, I feel the itch at the back of my skull, the same itch I felt right before my eyes started glitching so badly I could barely see my phone to call an Uber to take me to the hospital.

At least I made it into the car before my legs stopped working. Be thankful for small mercies.

I keep my eyes closed. I lay totally still. Don't give it anything to work with. Be empty, be nothing.

I float in an ocean of darkness, my breathing quiet and even, my mind blank, abandoned. The only sound is the hum of the fluorescent light.

The itch flares. Voices chatter in the hum. Phrases like bits of shrapnel fester to the surface of my memory.

"... widespread reports of fraud and malpractice have stunned ..."

"... unexpected bankruptcy is sending a shock wave through ..."

"... say they were misled about the nature of the agreement ..."

"... no scientific advancement without risk, say his defenders ..."

Beneath the chatter, the sound bites squawked from plastic faces, a chorus of voices rises, chanting. My mother's voice. My father's voice. My voice.

"What you deserve, what you deserve, what you deserve."

No. No one deserves this.

My head is a starless night curdled with accusations, a bottomless hole of guilt. Better the hell outside than the one within. I open my eyes. The holes in the acoustical tile whirl above me like Catherine wheels, spinning in the merciless gale of the pattern matcher. The loop's noose tightens around my brain. Somewhere nearby, an air conditioner shudders to life with a squeal of metal, a scream of terror.

The door shrieks open. The nursefather enters, followed by what can only be the doctor. The doctor stands at the foot of my bed and the loop swarms all over her, folding and stuttering, scrawling the face of a face on her face. The loop loops faces on her, a face coming out of her face.

"Mama," I say. "Mama, I'm so scared."

"I know you are," says motherdoctor. "I'm very sorry. I wish I had better news."

I think nursefather is crying. I think the air around him is full of tears.

"I've spoken to our legal department," she says. "As I'm sure you know, the ThinkingCap technology is privately owned and proprietary. Only licensed ThinkSmart technicians can legally perform maintenance."

I try to say something I don't know what I try to something. "I, I, I ..."

"Our IT and legal teams are pursuing every avenue," she she she says says. "The bankruptcy makes things especially difficult. The status of the intellectual property is uncertain. ThinkSmart's investors are very litigious. But the whole hospital is working as hard as we can on this."

"Get this thing," III sssaaayyy. "Get this thing."

"I'm truly, truly sorry about this. We're doing absolutely everything we can."

Nursefather smiles sadly says saying. "If they sue the hospital out of existence, that hurts a lot of people, right? A whole lot of people. What I mean to say is, we really appreciate the sacrifice you're making."

"Get this thing out."

Crumpling metal shreds the world, all space shatters like glass spiderwebbing the web of spider legs and fangs deep in my mind, where the I is. Motherfathernursedoctor flesh falls apart. Me, me, I did it. I did that.

"GET THIS THING OUT OF ME."

"We'll do everything we can to make sure you're as comfortable as possible." Voice of screen face smiling talking nonsense telling lies. Lying to my face to face my face. I'm glad you're dead. I'm glad I killed you.

The door is closing. The ceiling is spinning. Someone is screaming "GET THIS FUCKING THING OUT OF ME" and whoever it is they will not stop. Someone just keeps screaming.

Duet for Breath and Flame

I was sitting at home, trying to enjoy a quiet evening after a hectic day at work, when I suddenly felt sure I wasn't alone in the house. "Sara?" I said without thinking. "Are you there?" But of course she wasn't. She never would be. Across the living room, her smiling picture on the dusty piano was worse than nothing, a bitter mockery. I craved a voice, a touch, not an image. Not a cruel trick of my bereaved mind. I didn't want to remember her; I wanted her back.

Leaping up from the couch, I rushed out into the early evening. The faraway smoke of wildfire season scented the air. Gradually, as I wandered through the neighborhood, the whisper of summer leaves and the blandness of suburban lawns soothed my shrieking nerves, calmed my racing thoughts. I turned back, retraced my path.

I was a few blocks from home when a voice called to me from the shade of an oak. A child's voice, lisping and insistent. "Hey mister! You like music?"

I turned toward the call. Backlit by the glow of a half-curtained window, two children sat on folding chairs, a heap of gray shoeboxes at their feet. A posterboard sign was tacked to the oak's trunk, scrawled in spidery letters I couldn't make out.

The child on the left waved a delicate hand. "You like music, mister? You got a dollar?"

The pair had identical short haircuts, wore identical tie-dyed T-shirts. Green eyes shone from both faces, but the eyes on the left glittered eagerly to match a toothy grin, while the eyes on the right narrowed with distrust above a twisted scowl. Squinting at the posterboard sign, I managed to decipher its message: *HARPS $1 APIECE! BEAUTIFUL MUSIC AT AN UNBEATABLE PRICE!*

The grinning child snatched a shoebox from the heap and shook it in the air like a bag of treats. For another moment I hesitated, abashed by the scowling child's hostile stare, but curiosity won out. I crossed the lawn, entered the shade of the oak.

A whoop of triumph greeted me. "I knew it! I knew it! You like music, don't you, mister?"

The child's excitement was infectious. I laughed in the shadow. "Sure, I do. Who doesn't like music?"

"You got a dollar? You want to buy a harp?" The green eyes rolled upward, as if searching for a word scribbled on the underside of the leaves. "I'm Zephyr, by the way. Zephyr Flood. I'm eight years old. This is my brother, Brand."

"Pleased to meet you both," I said. I turned toward the face on the right, hoping to allay its suspicions. "And how old are you, Brand?"

Brand replied with an ursine grunt. Zephyr hissed from the corner of her mouth, "Be nice, you idiot! We're about to make a sale."

Brand heaved a dramatic sigh. "Eight," he mumbled. "Twins."

Zephyr flourished her shoebox in the air again. "You want to buy a harp, mister?"

I smiled. "It's a tempting offer, but I'm afraid I don't know how to play the harp."

"That's the best part! You don't need to know anything!" Crowing with laughter, she pulled the lid from the box. "Look!"

Inside the box sat a crude-looking contraption. Two thin boards an inch apart, attached at the corners with rusty nails. I lifted the thing by the edges, raising it to my eyes. Between the nails, spanning the gap between the boards, a web of strings glistened in the light from the half-curtained window.

"I've never seen a harp like this," I said.

Brand snorted. "Philistine," he muttered.

Zephyr swatted her brother's shoulder. "Be nice!"

Another weary sigh. "Like she said, anyone can play it." A disdainful sneer. "*Anyone.*"

"You use the wind to play it," Zephyr said. "I'll show you." She held her hands out flat. I placed the contraption across her palms.

Pursing her lips, she blew a stream of air between the boards. A silvery chord rose from the strings, intervals swelling and shifting as her breath swept through the gap. When her exhalation faltered, the tones faded one by one until the last low note evaporated in the smoke-tinged air.

Gooseflesh prickled my arms. It was the most beautiful music I'd ever heard. With trembling fingers, I fished a dollar from my pocket, and Brand snatched it away without a word.

Zephyr closed the lid over the harp and handed me the box. "Thanks, mister. Our daddy will be really happy we sold one."

A flash of motion in the corner of my eye drew my gaze to the glowing window. I glimpsed pale fingers curled around the curtain, a figure silhouetted against the glow. For a moment, other forms seemed to loom behind the silhouette, moving in time to music that hovered just at the threshold of hearing. Then the fingers uncurled, the figure vanished from the window, the music faded.

In the shade of the oak, the children's green eyes glittered. Zephyr grinned. "Good night, mister."

Brand scowled. "Night."

I hurried through the deepening twilight toward my empty house, the shoebox clutched to my chest, the jostled harp twanging and whimpering like a caged angel.

I woke to a high wind rattling my window. Outside, the moonlit trees swayed and shook, marionettes dancing to the play of invisible fingers.

The harp sat on the dresser beside my bed. Before going to sleep, I'd tried to coax music from it by blowing into the gap, but the most I could conjure was a sad, discordant groan, like the wheeze of a trampled harmonica.

Rising from bed, I carried the harp through the dark house and into the backyard, where the grass I hadn't mowed in weeks rippled and thrashed. The wind swirled around me, hot and dry, acrid with charred wood and a simmering chemical overtone. Somewhere out of sight, the world was burning.

I stepped barefoot into the unkempt grass. Lifting the harp in my hands, I offered its strings to the gale. If I couldn't play it, the wind surely could.

Music filled the yard, unfurling in streaming banners of sound from the space between the boards. Each shift of the smoky air called forth a new combination, one moment a gleaming circle of perfect fifths, the next a seething cacophony of stacked semitones. A gust tossed a volley of leaf litter through the gap, punctuating the notes with a percussive clatter of pings and clangs. The beauty of it all made my head whirl.

The gale rose higher still, the strings wailing in a manic crescendo. The inch of space that separated the boards was the spasming valve of the universe, the tortured aperture through which all things flowed. Out of that narrow throat, the wind shrieked its joy and terror, a molten wail pouring from lungs of fire.

No—it wasn't the wind that shrieked. It was a voice I recognized. The harp fell from my numb fingers, rattled in the shaggy grass.

"Sara?" I turned in a circle, scanning the moon-bright grass, the yard's dark corners. "Sara? Sara?"

No one there. No shape, no voice. Just another wretched, pointless memory.

Hopelessness kindled to fury. I raised my foot to crush the harp, to stomp the lying thing to splinters. What held me back was a sudden memory—a child's hand, snatching a dollar from my grasp. I'd paid good money for this thing! Damned if I'd let two little brats fleece me. At the very least, I owed it to myself to make an effort.

The wind wrapped me in a smoky shroud. I felt very tired, exhausted beyond bearing. I picked up the harp and went back into the house.

The next evening, I sat in the living room with the harp in my hands. All day I'd been like a man in a trance, my body going through the motions at work while my thoughts circled around my strange solo concert in the backyard. The gale, the music, the voice. Amazement and terror and despair danced patterns in my mind until finally, in the car on the way home, everything resolved into a simple octave of clarity.

What had gone wrong, wrecked the performance? Sheer hubris. I'd aimed too high too fast, like a child sitting down at a piano for the first time and trying to play Rachmaninoff. When Zephyr Flood said I didn't need to know anything, that was just patter, a clever sales pitch. Everything takes skill, knowledge, discipline. Practice, practice, practice.

I raised the harp to my face, blew into the gap.

Nothing.

I closed my eyes, focused my thoughts. *Breathe in. Feel the breath filling your lungs, charging you with purpose.* I pursed my lips. I opened my eyes. *Breathe out.*

Softly, tentatively, a note took shape. As I exhaled, the note swelled high and pure, a plaintive cry in a world of silence.

Tap, tap.

A knock at the door. I lowered the harp. The note broke off with a dying sob.

Tap, tap, tap.

On the porch stood a short, slight man, his dark suit too big for his frame. Behind his thick glasses, green eyes glittered. He smiled. "Good evening. I hope I'm not disturbing you."

"Not at all," I said. "What can I do for you?"

"For me? Oh, nothing at all for me. This is just a friendly visit. A follow-up, you might say, to gauge customer satisfaction." A slim hand darted into the folds of his oversized jacket. "I believe my little ones have conducted some business with you." Reappearing, the hand extended a small white card.

♫ GAIUS FLOOD, LUTHIER/PNEUMATOLOGIST ♫
CUSTOM INSTRUMENTS ♫ PRICES NEGOTIABLE ♫

I took the card, shook the hand. "Charlie Seeger," I said. "Pleased to meet you. I have to say, Mr. Flood, that daughter of yours is quite a salesperson."

"Yes, Zephyr's really taken to it. And Brand? What was your impression of him?"

"He, um ... well, he seemed a bit less interested in closing the transaction."

Mr. Flood chuckled. "You're very polite. Brand can be quite the little dickens. Don't read too much into his sales demeanor, though. He's a sweetheart, just like his sister. They play that good-cop bad-cop routine to create a little drama, draw the customer in."

"It worked on me, I suppose." The twins' faces rose in my mind, one grinning, one scowling. *You like music, mister?* I frowned. "It's funny, though ... I don't remember telling your children where I live. How did you know where to find me?"

"Well, they were both so excited about the sale, they couldn't stop talking about it. You should have heard them, so proud of themselves, going over every little detail. What they'd said, what you'd said. What you look like. The sound of your voice. Those little brains of theirs are regular tar pits, holding onto everything, keeping it all preserved. By the time they were finished, I couldn't help but recognize you. Just from seeing you around the neighborhood, you know, here and there. My family's lived here a long time. We know everybody, all the comings and go-ings."

He paused, his eyes downcast for a moment. "On that note, let me just say how sorry I was to hear … well. It's a dreadful thing." He raised his left hand, as if swearing an oath. Along with a silver band, the fourth finger bore a loop of black ribbon tied with a tiny bow. "I understand how terrible it is. Losing someone."

I couldn't speak, couldn't react. Memories rose up, memo-ries I didn't want—Sara's voice, her laugh, her love of music. Blinking back tears, I stared over Mr. Flood's shoulder. A gust of wind shook the maple in my front yard; a pungent whiff of smoke filled my nostrils.

"Ah … CHOO!"

My sneeze broke the spell. Sniffling, hands cupped over my nose and mouth, I said, "I'd better get a tissue. Tell your children thank you. Tell them I'm enjoying the harp."

Mr. Flood nodded. "I'll be sure to let them know." At the edge of the porch, he turned back. "If you ever need someone to talk to, you know where to find me." He stepped into the wind, his jacket billowing.

⁘

Mr. Flood's visit left me anxious, uneasy. What did he mean, he'd seen me "here and there"? I was positive I'd never met him or his children before yesterday. I must have passed that house a hundred times, but I'd never known who lived there, or if anyone lived there at all. Yet he knew what I looked like, and where I lived, and about Sara ... those green eyes, that slender hand disappearing beneath a too-large jacket ... that black ribbon on his finger, displayed like a secret sign ...

It all kept whirling around in my head. I couldn't sleep. At first, I tried to calm my nerves by practicing the harp in the living room, but as the notes rose and fell, the back of my neck began to tingle, as if a stream of breath were coursing through the house. I felt that if I tried to stand up, I'd find myself entangled in a labyrinth of strings; if I raised my eyes from the harp, I'd see that my house was a narrow gap between two thin boards; if I turned my head, I'd see green eyes glittering in darkness, white teeth shining in a mouth that grinned and scowled at once, and behind the teeth a writhing red tongue, the folds of a hideous throat.

It was better in the backyard. No walls for memories to get trapped in. I sprawled on the lawn with the harp in my hands, teaching myself new notes. I felt calm, almost happy. I was learning the instrument one string at a time, shaping my breath to its contours. As each tone faded in the darkness, my sense of accomplishment grew.

I decided to challenge myself. With the tip of my tongue between my lips, I split my breath into two channels, stirring two strings to produce a simple chord. A minor third floated in the stillness, fragile and mournful.

Such a small thing, yet it felt triumphant, a conquest. Rising from the grass, I hoisted the harp above my head like a trophy.

From somewhere in the night, another chord rang out, and all my pride vanished, transformed into astonishment. It was the same minor third I'd played, but where my tones were weak and quavery—a beginner's strained achievement—these were bold, long-drawn, with the stylish verve of true mastery.

The chord sang on, steady as the polestar. Subtleties emerged, shifts of color and timbre that only a virtuoso could achieve. I began to sense a personality in the music, a soul animating its nuances. A mouth took shape from the notes, the lips and tongue that orchestrated the breath. Eyes opened above the mouth, bright with the thrill of invention. A face shone in my mind, the face of the master harper beaming with joy, with forgiveness, a face I'd give anything to see in the flesh again, anything ...

Frenzied, I raced across the yard, through the house, down the street. By the time I reached the end of the block, the music had disappeared, but I knew where it had come from. I ran through the neighborhood with the harp in my hand, my fingers hooked around the cold, rough nails.

The window that had shone so bright was now washed in a feeble glow, like a television's flicker spilling from another room. In the oak's pitch-black shadow, the posterboard sign floated dim and ghostly, the writing completely illegible.

I stood on the porch, gathering my courage. Two deep breaths, in and out. There was no doorbell, only an ugly knocker shaped like a musical note. Shifting the harp to my other hand, I knocked three times.

Tap, tap, tap.

The sound reminded me of Mr. Flood on my doorstep, his business card and his glittering eyes and his air of secret knowledge. His black-ribboned finger, his offer of sympathy. The memory filled me with rage. Who was he to come to my house, to keep tabs on my life, to claim he understood? Whatever he knew, whatever he was, how could he possibly understand? I seized the knocker again, slammed it against the metal plate.

The note snapped off in my hand. Startled, I dropped it. It hit the porch with a tinny clink.

My anger turned to chagrin. What was I doing? I'd heard music from the darkness, I'd imagined a face, and now I was pounding on someone's door after midnight, breaking their knocker! I stepped off the porch, craned my neck to look through the window. As far as I could see, the room was completely bare. Blank walls and naked floorboards wavered in the flickering light.

Staring into the empty room, I accepted the truth. What I'd been seeking wasn't there, wasn't anywhere anymore. A dead face, dead lips, dead eyes ... only fragments, figments, empty memories. The real Sara might as well never have existed.

Walking away from the house, I paused beside the oak. I hefted the harp in my hand, stuck a fingertip into the gap between the boards. A string poked my flesh, cold and sharp.

I tossed the harp into the shadows with a grunt. It clanged softly in the grass at the base of the tree.

Among the branches, a pair of eyes opened, green and glowing in the abyss of black foliage. Leaves rustled as a lithe figure dropped from the tree to the ground.

Fear tightened my throat, froze my limbs. I stood petrified at the edge of the shadow.

The figure crouched low. Its eyes cast a pool of soft radiance where the harp lay on its side, half-shrouded in the long grass. In the reflection of the eyes' glow, I glimpsed the outlines of the crouching form. It seemed unfinished, viscous, like a wax doll taken too early from the mold.

"Zephyr?" I whispered. "Brand?"

Rising, the figure turned its eyes to the oak's trunk. It pointed a fingerless blob of a hand at the sign that hung there, illuminated in the soft green light. The words I'd read before had been crossed out, a new message scrawled beneath them in the same spidery letters. *SOLD OUT! NO REFUNDS!*

I shook my head. "It's fine. Keep the dollar." I turned back toward the street.

From behind me, a voice murmured sadly, "Don't you like music after all, mister?"

I hurried away through the darkness. By the time I got home, a rising wind had filled the neighborhood with the tang of smoke.

The next morning, I felt surprisingly calm. I whistled a jaunty tune on my way to the office, went through the day's tasks with an easygoing smile. Not even a news alert about wildfires in the next county could sour my mood. I felt like I'd escaped from a dungeon.

When I got home from work, a high wind was coursing down the street. A gust peppered my face with grit, and I covered my eyes with my hands as I ran for the porch. Blinking the bits of dust away, I saw what lay on my doorstep.

A gray shoebox, tied crosswise with a black ribbon.

I prodded it with my toe. No jangle of strings, only a tinny rattle.

I took the box into the house. Opening it, I found the snapped-off musical note from the Floods' door, bedded in cotton like a pet bird's corpse. Beside the ugly knocker lay a folded sheet of paper—a message, handwritten in green ink.

Dear Charlie,

In view of your bereaved and disordered state, I forgive you the destruction of this knocker, though it holds great value for me, having been designed, smelted and cast by my departed better half. What I can less easily forgive is your ingratitude, and making Zephyr and Brand cry, but the tender-hearted darlings have prevailed on me to offer you a second chance. My family is giving a concert tonight, featuring a piece of my talented little ones' own composition. Your attendance is politely but firmly requested.

Your friend, Gaius

P.S. She will be there.

I stared at the paper for a long time before refolding it, putting it back in the shoebox. I picked up the broken knocker, flicked it with a fingernail. It rang like a bell, a clear tone that seemed to shatter as it faded, one note splitting into two, ten, a thousand, filling the house with a vapor of music.

I lay down on the couch. I closed my eyes.

———◦———

Sirens jolted me awake. The night was full of noise. The wind roared, motors growled in the street, feedback squealed from a loudspeaker as a voice yelled, "This is a mandatory evacuation! Leave now! Bring only essential items!"

Groggy and disoriented, I rose from the couch. Essential items? Nonsense. Nothing was essential. I patted my pocket—keys still there. I staggered to the front door.

Cars were streaming down the street, fleeing destruction. All along the block, trees shook in the hot wind like prisoners praying for mercy. A siren whooped nearby, and an amplified voice wallowed in static.

The sky was clotted with darkness. In the distance, the clouds glowed red.

I dug the keys from my pocket, unlocked the car. Reflected in the window, I saw myself reach for the door handle, saw my own eyes full of fear. But what was there to fear? What to escape from? What fate could be worse than what I'd already suffered?

She will be there.

Smoke-thickened air scoured my face as I walked slowly past the wind-tortured lawns, against the flow of escaping traffic.

The oak tree flailed, the posterboard sign gone. A line of watery light showed where the Floods' front door stood ajar. Pushing it open, I called into the house, "Mr. Flood? Gaius?"

Silence.

"Zephyr? Brand?"

Silence.

"... Sara?"

No sense turning back now. I stepped across the threshold, eased the door shut behind me.

I stood in a narrow room that ran the length of the house. The space was as empty as it had seemed the night before, lit with the same unsteady glow. The light glinted from a doorway at the far end of the room, and as I crossed the dust-coated floorboards, I strained my ears to listen for movement, voices, anything. Nothing.

Through the flickering doorway, I entered a long, wide chamber, longer and wider than the house should have allowed. The walls were hung with musical instruments, violins and trumpets, cellos and flutes and horns, enough to equip an orchestra. Other instruments lay strewn around the floor, half-finished and unrecognizable, their rough-hewn frames bristling with reeds and strings that cast long, thin shadows in the wavering light.

I followed the glow to a rectangular window in the wall opposite the doorway. Behind a thick pane, bluish-white flames danced and coiled around shapeless, molten-looking lumps. Some sort of kiln or foundry, where Mr. Flood forged his custom instruments. The glass must have been tempered to an incredible strength; not a breath of heat escaped the furnace, not a whisper of sound. The flames seemed as chilly and silent as a photograph, a hollow apparition of living fire.

I gazed into the furnace, waiting, listening. Nothing. Had I been stood up? Was it a prank of some kind, a punishment for my sins? Maybe the Floods were waiting for me in another room, behind a door I hadn't seen. I turned, scanning the chamber. No way out except the door I'd come through.

She will be there.

What choice did I have but to believe it? What else was left for me? Turning back toward the glass, I repeated the words in my mind until they acquired a cadence, a rise and fall. *She will be there. She will be there.* I nodded my head to the phrase's rhythm. I whistled its melody.

Behind the window, an eye opened, glittering green among the pale flames.

My throat clenched, cutting off my whistling. Choking and gasping, I stumbled backward, away from the furnace.

Another eye opened behind the glass, another, another. Wisps of fire curled into mouths that grinned, mouths that scowled. Further back, in the belly of the forge, a host of writhing forms emerged, radiant bodies twisting and flowing.

Transfixed, I stared into the surging chaos. I saw faces taking shape from human magma, an endless crowd of faces, and among the throng, one face I'd know anywhere, a pair of unforgettable eyes blazing with agony, terror, love.

Delicate hands pressed against the glass. A wave of heat crashed over me as the furnace began to open from the inside. All the odors of an ignited world swirled around me, smoke and hot metal and melted plastic and burning hair.

The unforgettable face in the depths of the forge opened its mouth to scream. Between its lips gleamed a network of strings, more strings than I could have imagined, criss-crossing the gap in amazing profusion. When the scream came, it came as a torrent of song that blasted the furnace's window open, sent a gale of flame howling through the room. I felt myself hurtling through vast spaces, borne on wings of white-hot melody up into the Flood house's dark altitudes.

Ten slender hands seized each of mine. A thousand shining faces whirled around me, grinning and scowling, and even the scowling faces had green eyes that glittered sweetly, wept emerald tears of joy.

A choir of triumphant voices trilled in my ear, "We *knew* you liked music, mister!"

Below me, I saw the neighborhood spread out like a burning map, orange billows sweeping in on the wind to devour the neat patterns of houses. Windows bursting, roofs collapsing, trees exploding as their sap boiled—the whole inferno drummed a percussive counterpoint to the column of song erupting into the sky. All the instruments from Gaius Flood's workshop spun in the fiery cyclone, every string and key joining the universal chorus.

We soared and sang all night as the neighborhood burned. At last, when the wave of fire swept on and only ash remained, the column sank back into the darkness of the house. The unburnt walls rose to embrace us as we hurtled back into the workshop and down the forge's throat. Molten arms enfolded me, molten lips pressed mine. I felt my flesh soften and flow, my thoughts and memories dissolve, and as I sank into the mass with the others, I wondered what songs Mr. Flood would fashion from me.

Wheel of Meat

The universe is a wheel of meat. I keep it in my basement. Wanna have a look?

Check it out! Barbed-wire spokes branch from a skull hub to end in spikes upon which the skewered meat flails and dances. With every turn of the wheel, a trillion lives flourish, wither and rot. That's the universe.

You're skeptical, I can tell. I don't blame you. But look—that oozing gobbet there, twitching on its spike, carried around by the spinning wheel. Notice anything familiar about it?

That tortured, festering glob, whirling helpless ... that's you! Just listen, it's screaming in your voice.

Smoochfest

It seemed like every time Vernon left his apartment, that couple from the other end of the hall was there, smooching. When he checked his mail, they were smooching next to the mailboxes, pressed up against the wall, the woman clutching the man's shoulders. When he took out the trash, they were smooching outside the little room with the garbage chute, the man's fingers buried in the woman's hair. If they weren't smooching in the lobby when Vernon left for work, the tiles echoing with their lips' smacking and slurping, they'd be smooching in the elevator when he came home, squeaking and whimpering and shoving their tongues down each other's throats.

Vernon was no prude. He preferred to mind his own business, thank you very much. But in the month since the couple moved in, he'd witnessed more smooching than in all the rest of his forty-six years on earth, and it was getting on his nerves. Maybe he'd have felt differently if the couple was movie-star gorgeous, but they were both so average-looking that when they weren't right in front of him, smooching, he couldn't even remember what they looked like. All he could picture were two pairs of lips mashed together, moving hungrily.

Vernon had never said more than "Good morning" and "Good evening" to anyone else in the building, but now, whenever he ran into another resident, he asked if they'd noticed anything strange about the new couple.

"Strange how?" said the old woman who lived on the floor above him. The two of them stood in the lobby, waiting for the elevator.

"Like how they're smooching all the time, for everyone to see!" Vernon grimaced, the lips writhing in his mind.

"Oh, they're just a pair of young lovebirds." The old woman chuckled. "Give them a year or two, they'll be as miserable as the rest of us."

When the elevator doors opened, the whoosh of air sounded like a passionate gasp. Vernon winced, covered his ears with his hands.

"Have a good night," the old woman said as Vernon stepped out of the elevator. He didn't reply, his thoughts consumed by the spectacle that was sure to greet him, but his floor was empty and silent for once. No bodies entwined against the door to the emergency stairwell, no wordless murmurs, no moist lips squelching. Just the beige-carpeted hallway, with his apartment at one end and the couple's apartment at the other.

Someone had to bring them to their senses. Get them to show a little decency. Vernon stalked down the hallway.

In front of the couple's door, he paused to gather his resolve. Best to begin with a firm knock, let them know he was serious. He raised his fist.

The door trembled in its frame.

Vernon froze, his fist suspended in air. Were they watching him through the peephole? Were they shaking the door to taunt him, daring him to make his priggish complaint?

The door trembled again. Vernon heard a faint rustling, wet and organic, like a hand swirling in raw hamburger.

A wave of revulsion shuddered through him. The couple was pressing against the other side of the door, less than two feet from his face, smooching.

Sounds ebbed and flowed. Strangled moans, convulsive sighs. Repellent suctions, thirsty gurgles. Every few seconds, the door quivered—never the rhythmic thump of intercourse, always the spasmodic frenzy of a vehement smooch. If the couple had been fucking on the other side of the door, that would have been something Vernon could understand. Something normal, bearable. But they weren't fucking.

They never fuck, Vernon thought. *They only smooch.* Somehow the idea terrified him, filled him with the dread of some unholy revelation.

His fist was still raised, still poised to knock on the door, but the blood had drained from his hand, leaving it cold and numb. How long had he been listening there? Minutes, hours?

He lowered his arm. Pins and needles flooded his flesh. Shivering and panting, he hurried down the hallway to his own apartment, the horrible noises fading behind him.

When Vernon left for work the next morning, the hallway was empty again. Waiting for the elevator, he thought he heard hungry mouths squirming, but when he turned his head toward the couple's apartment, the sound stopped. By the time he reached the lobby, he'd convinced himself he'd imagined it.

That evening, though, the sound was undeniably there, slithering moistly along the beige carpet. He whistled a tune to drown it out, but he couldn't keep the images from forming in his mind. Puckered lips pressing, curled tongues twisting. Mouths crushed together, wriggling like red grubs. He squeezed his eyes shut.

Vernon awoke with a start. He sat confused in bed, wondering what had disturbed him, until he noticed the noises drifting through his apartment, low but unmistakable. Wet, meaty, hideous.

He looked at the clock. 3:17 AM.

I'll never escape it, he thought. *It'll follow me everywhere.*

He went to the kitchen, poured himself a glass of water. The faucet hissed like breath through moistened lips. As he drank, a lustful gulping filled his ears. The water thrust a cold tongue down his throat. With a spasm of rage, he threw the glass into the sink. Shards clattered and chimed.

When the shards lay still, a sudden calm fell on him, a pall of certainty. He opened a drawer and took out a knife, the big butcher knife he almost never used. He'd sometimes wondered why he'd bought it, why he kept it around. Now he knew. Now was the time.

Time to put an end to this infernal smoochfest.

The noises grew louder as Vernon strode down the hallway. The door to the couple's apartment was ajar, the deadbolt shining against the jamb like a silver tongue. As if they'd propped the door open for a brief excursion, but forgot to retract the bolt when they returned, in their haste to resume smooching.

Or, Vernon thought, as if they were expecting him. As if he was their long-awaited guest.

He slowly opened the door, slowly entered. In the living room, an arc lamp glowed dimly over a black leather couch. The couple sprawled on the couch, arms entangled, faces squashed together, their movements making the leather squeal a staccato accompaniment to the cacophony of smacks, gulps and gasps that filled the apartment.

The couple's upper bodies undulated with constant motion—torsos swiveling, heads turning, hands stroking and gripping—but below the waist, they were totally, terribly still. It was as though their lower parts existed in another world, a world so utterly chaste it was obscene. Seeing their bodies freakishly split between infinite abandon and infinite restraint, Vernon thought he might vomit.

Instead, he ran to the couch and plunged his knife into the man's neck. Blood showered the black leather as the man slumped sideways and rolled to the floor. The man stared up at Vernon, his average-looking face absolutely expressionless. Only his blood-coated lips moved, puckering, twisting.

The woman's eyes widened, shining in the lamplight. Vernon stabbed her in the throat, and another cascade of blood spilled on the leather. The woman crumpled forward and fell in a heap across the man's legs.

The knife dropped from Vernon's blood-slick hand. He staggered backward against the wall. He knew he'd done the right thing, rid the world of some awful monstrosity, but he hadn't expected so much blood.

The couple lay on the floor, their arms twitching. No, not just twitching—reaching, feebly grasping. As Vernon watched in horror, the woman pulled herself inch by inch along the man's body. The man took the woman by the shoulders, drew her blank, average-looking face toward his. They wrapped their shaking arms around each other. They pressed their mouths together, tongues sliding between wet, red lips. They smooched.

Unsteady, bewildered, Vernon pushed away from the wall. He picked up the knife. Only a sense of obligation, of duty to the world as he understood it, held his mind together as he separated the man and the woman—harder than he'd expected, the lips clinging as if magnetized—and cut their bodies apart. He cut their grasping arms off and threw each one in a different corner. He cut their smooching lips off, cut their probing tongues out, carried the lips and tongues to the bathroom and flushed them down the toilet. He cut their heads off, dropped one in the bathtub, the other in the kitchen sink. It took a lot of slicing, hacking, tearing. By the time he was done, it was almost dawn.

Leaving, Vernon retracted the deadbolt and shut the door. He stumbled, bloody and exhausted, back to his end of the hall. After a long, hot shower, he collapsed into bed.

It was afternoon when he awoke. He lay staring at the ceiling, trying to decide if what he'd seen, what he'd done, had been real or a dream.

He was still thinking about it when he heard the sounds. Shuffling steps in the living room, and something else. A sliding sound.

It was a dream, Vernon thought. *I'm still dreaming.* But goosebumps were rising along his arms, and his teeth began to chatter.

The bedroom door, which he'd left cracked, began to swing wider, the hinges emitting a high, soft creak. When the door was half-open, something entered, sliding slowly along the floor, too low to see from the bed. Another thing slid in after it, then another and another.

It's a dream, Vernon thought. His heart raced, his breath came fast and shallow.

The door opened wider. Vernon pressed his hands over his eyes for a moment, but whatever was there, it would be worse not to know, worse to fear without seeing. He uncovered his eyes.

Two bodies entered the bedroom. Two bloody trunks, armless, headless. They stood just inside the door, not approaching the bed, as if they were standing guard.

It's a dream, Vernon thought. His eyes bulged, straining against their sockets.

One by one, the sliding things came to rest beside the bed.

Worse not to know. Vernon sat up, looked over the edge.

Four arms lay on the floor, hands extended toward him, ragged shoulders pointing away. The first arm gripped the woman's head by the hair. The second gripped the man's. The two heads lay on their sides, lipless mouths grinning, eyes fixed on Vernon's face.

It's a dream, Vernon thought. His head whirled. He felt himself falling.

Cupped in the third arm's palm, two tongues squirmed and tangled like newborn puppies. The fourth hand was empty. Thin trails of blood led away from it, toward the bed.

It's a dream. It's a dream.

The sheets at the foot of the bed rustled and shook. He looked down.

His first thought was that two red worms were crawling up over the edge of the bed, gripping the sheets in their coils. But they weren't worms, of course.

The two pairs of lips crawled over the sheets, across his feet, up his legs. Vernon was paralyzed with terror, with disbelief.

The lips left smears of blood behind as they advanced up his stomach, up his chest, toward his face.

"It's a dream," Vernon whispered. Beneath his pulse's thunder, he heard the icy crack of his mind breaking apart.

"It's not a dream," the two pairs of lips said in unison. They spoke with the same voice, gentle, toneless, wafting from a throat of air.

The lips crawled up the sides of his neck, onto his cheeks. One pair probed the corner of his mouth tenderly, delicately. The other was more forceful, pressing with fierce passion.

Vernon couldn't speak. No breath would come. Only his moving mouth shaped the words.

"It's a dream."

The lips pushed hard against him, two mouths on his at once. Vernon felt his own lips begin to answer the pressure, to writhe, to smooch, and as the fragments of his shattered mind plunged into an abyss where sacred lechery locks vile celibacy in an eternal embrace, he heard the couple's single voice, felt their phantom breath flood his mouth.

"It's better than a dream," the couple said. "It's a kiss."

Dreamland Coffee

The way the light gleams on Evan's face looks strange. April can't tell if he's smiling or scowling. He's sitting on the couch in the living room of their apartment with a mug of coffee in his hand.

"Look who finally decided to get up," Evan says.

"Is it that late?" April says.

"It's almost noon, sleepyhead." A wisp of steam curls up from his mug, spiraling and shimmering in the strange light.

April goes to the kitchen to pour herself some coffee. The mug she grabs from the drying rack has a picture of a kitten on it, a curled-up, sleeping kitten with a thought bubble over its head. The thought bubble holds the kitten's dream: a steaming mug of coffee. The mug in the dream has another kitten on it, or maybe it's the same kitten, April can't tell. The kitten on the mug in the dream has a strange light gleaming on it.

She sits on the couch next to Evan. It's not just the light gleaming on his face; the face itself looks strange, different. The skin is too smooth, the pores too small, everything too tight against the skull.

"You look a little bleary," Evan says. "Like you didn't sleep real well."

"Oh." She doesn't know what else to say. His face is too close to the skull.

"You were tossing and turning all night. You kept moaning in your sleep. Bad dreams?"

"Maybe." April never remembers her dreams. She looks at her mug, where a kitten dreams of coffee and a kitten and a strange light. "I need a shower," she says.

By the time she's showered and dressed, Evan is gone. He often goes out without telling her where he's headed. Alone in the apartment, April drifts to the window. The sky is wintry, full of clouds. She sips her coffee. It's gone lukewarm, and the blend isn't her favorite. It smells vaguely like licorice. An oily scum floats on the surface, glinting rainbows in the strange light. Maybe it's the kitten's dream glinting. She drinks the coffee, scum and all. Not for the first time, she wonders if she could get work as a barista, or if she'd be rejected as "overqualified." The dream slides down her throat. *Maybe I should go back to sleep,* she thinks.

A buzz shears the air, startling her. She hurries across the room to her desk, where her phone rests on a heap of notebooks full of intricate diagrams, relics of her useless graduate degree. The kitten's dream curls in her stomach.

The green bubble on the phone holds a message from Evan. *hey i'm at the coffee shop around the corner. something bad is happening. can you come down and meet me please.*

She sighs. No going back to sleep, then. She slips the phone into her pocket, puts on her jacket.

When the elevator arrives, two people are already in it, their bodies buried in heavy coats and scarves. They ride silently down behind April, dim reflections wavering in the metal door. One of the reflections is taller than the other, but that's the only difference April can see.

Halfway down, the tall one breaks the silence. "Isn't it just awful, what's happening?"

"Awful, awful," says the other.

"They say it's coming from all over."

"Horrible, horrible."

The elevator is taking a long time. It always takes a long time—it's an old elevator, clinging to old cables in an old build-ing—but it's taking even longer than usual, inching down the shaft like a too-large mouthful sliding slowly down a long, nar-row throat. The thought makes April's stomach turn.

"You look like you could use some more coffee," says the tall one.

April waits for the other to say something. The two reflec-tions waver, distorted in the dim light of the elevator.

Something presses down on her shoulder.

"I said, you look like you could use some more coffee," says the tall one.

April's heart beats faster. Her throat clenches. A pale hand is gleaming on her shoulder, pressing down through her coat, its tall fingers curling into the hollow above her collarbone.

Long fingers, she thinks. *Fingers are long, not tall*. But these fingers, pale and curling in the dim light, are tall, not long, as if space and its directions are curling with the fingers, twisting and folding. A diagram begins to take shape in April's mind. *The x-axis*, she thinks, *and the y-axis*. And the mysterious z-axis, shooting off at a crazy angle into a direction no diagram can show.

"Dimension," says the other.

"What?" April says. Her voice croaks in her clenched throat.

"Dimension, not direction," says the other.

"Ah, don't worry about it. This one's all right," says the tall one. The pale hand rises and falls, patting her on the shoulder. She sees a smile reflected in the door, or something like a smile. Something white and gleaming. Her heart races like a star whirling around a black hole.

The elevator shudders to a stop. The tall fingers uncurl. April steps out into the lobby, nearly sobbing with relief.

The two quickly pass her as they stride across the empty lobby, the tall one striding faster. When the tall one turns at the end of the lobby to wait for the other, April glimpses something like a face, something pale with dim holes, its outline wavering in the strange light that gleams into the lobby from outside.

The other reaches the end of the lobby. "Thought you'd never make it," the tall one says.

"What's the hurry?" the other says. "It's all coming together."

When they're gone, tears of relief swarm in April's eyes, blurring the lobby. She's almost glad to have come down in the elevator with those two, the joy of their absence is so delicious.

The joyful moment passes. She remembers why she came down. Evan is down here, at the coffee shop around the corner, where something bad is happening. Not just bad but awful, horrible.

Outside, the light gleams all around. April can't tell where it's coming from. The clouds glint rainbows overhead, swirling like an oily scum. The sidewalk is strewn with shiny grains that crunch under her feet, maybe salt to melt the snow that was supposed to fall overnight but didn't, or maybe the grains are seeds from which tendrils of light sprouted while April was dreaming bad dreams she can't remember. Anything's possible. The light could be beaming out of windows, certain windows along the street that shimmer strangely as if the panes are turning, spiraling in their frames as the light beams through. The light must be coming from somewhere. Everything comes from somewhere. But where? Where?

The question so consumes April's mind that, when a door opens in the sidewalk ahead of her, she almost walks right into it. She stumbles backward, startled by her narrow escape.

The door is a reddish-gray leaf of rusted metal. It folds up and over, crashes against the sidewalk. The smell of damp concrete and rotting vegetables billows up from below as a shining orb, a head, appears in the doorway, tendrils of gleaming dark hair plastered across its brow. The head rises, followed by broad shoulders and bulging arms that cradle an overstuffed trash bag. Heavy shoes clang on metal stairs. The bag sloshes with every step.

The person rising from the doorway shines wetly all over, as if they've been lying in a vat of grease. Strings of viscous liquid drip from their nose, the tips of their ears, the elbows of their gray coveralls crooked under the sloshing bag. Bubbles swell and pop at the corners of their lips as their mouth puckers and they begin to whistle a playful tune. With one foot on the sidewalk, the other resting on a stair, the shining person swings their arms and heaves the trash bag into the gutter.

A dry, raspy voice calls up from below. "Hey, what's with the whistling?"

"I dunno," the shining person says, their voice light and pleasant. "I guess I just got a song in my heart."

"Well, get back down here, songbird. It's happening again." The dry voice crumbles into a fit of coughing. Whoever's down there sounds either very old or very sick, or both. Desiccated.

"Ahhh," the shining person groans. Their voice, so light and pleasant a moment ago, now oozes with such loathing and disgust that, standing a few steps away on the sidewalk, April shudders, horrified at the thought that the stream of pure revulsion bubbling from the shining person's mouth might turn on her.

Instead, the groaning voice falls silent. The only sound is a faint trickling from the gutter, where something dark and oily dribbles from a hole in the trash bag. The shining person turns to go back down the stairs, their shimmering face swiveling toward April, who lowers her eyes to the sidewalk, afraid to be caught staring.

"Sorry," the shining person says.

A jolt of alarm snaps April's head up. Are they talking to her? What do they want?

The shining person stands frozen in mid-turn. No, not quite frozen—they're shivering, quaking in terror. The viscous liquid ripples with the vibration, swirling like a fabric of whirlpools on the person's skin. Stitched on the breast pocket of their coveralls, a cloth patch shows a curled-up, sleeping kitten gleaming in a strange light, the thought bubble over the kitten's head full of churning, oily darkness. The kitten is having a nightmare.

"I'm sorry," the shining person says. Their eyes are wide, radiant with fear. "I was blocking your path. I apologize."

If I accept their apology, they'll leave me alone, April thinks. "It's fine."

The shining person closes their eyes and breathes a huge sigh, droplets ballooning like baby spiders from their lips. April's never seen anyone look so relieved.

"Hey!" the dry voice calls up from below. "What's going on up there? Enjoying the view? Solving the crossword, maybe? Get down here and do your job! It's coming from all over. I'm not dealing with this by myself."

The shining person sighs again, shakes their head. They lick their lips with a wide, deep tongue that looks like it could stretch all the way up to their forehead. The metal stairs clang as they descend.

Long tongue. Wide, long tongue. But no. Deep. The diagram spins in April's mind, the x- and y-axes racing, spiraling around each other. The z-axis whirls madly.

Halfway down the stairs, the shining person pauses. "Don't take this the wrong way," they say, "but you look like you could use some more coffee."

April forces a smile. "I'm actually on my way to the coffee shop right now."

The shining person nods. "Glad to hear it. I guess it's all coming together." They disappear beneath the sidewalk.

Another delicious absence. Another moment of joy comes and goes. Evan is still at the coffee shop around the corner, where something awful is still happening, or something horrible is happening again. *Why did he ask me to come meet him, anyway? Why didn't he just come back to the apartment?* It's true that Evan often does foolish things without thinking. He often asks her to do foolish things, too. *But usually I just tell him to stop being ridiculous. Why not this time?* Maybe because of the kitten's dream curling in her stomach. *I could use some more coffee.*

She hurries down the block. Beside her, the gutter oozes with whatever's leaking from the trash bag, a dark, swirling flow that smells like nutmeg. She keeps going, the strange light gleaming around her, the salt or seeds crunching on the sidewalk, the dark flow oozing, the windows turning and shimmering.

Rounding the corner, she finds the door of the coffee shop flung wide, held open by a thin rubber doorstop. A sign taped to the glass reads NOW HIRING, ALL POSITIONS AVAIL-ABLE.

She stands in the middle of the shop and looks around for Evan. The little tables are crowded with people clutching paper cups, leaning their heads together, filling the shop with whispers. At the back of the shop, two baristas in gray aprons stand behind the counter, one beside the cash register and one beside the espresso machine. Evan is nowhere to be seen.

She slips her phone out of her pocket. No calls, no messages. All around, the leaning heads whisper.

Evan picks up on the third ring. "Hello?"

"Hey, I'm here," she says. "Where are you?"

"What do you mean? I'm here. Where are you?"

"I'm at the coffee shop."

In the pause before Evan speaks, she hears whistling over the phone. Wherever Evan is, someone else is there with him, whistling a playful tune.

"Oh, I get it," he says. "You're at the other coffee shop."

"What are you talking about? What other coffee shop?"

"Look, it's fine. I'll come to where you are."

She hangs up.

The playful tune is still there, weaving among the whispers. The whistling must not have been coming from the phone, after all. In the strange light pouring through the open door, the tables look too small, the whispering heads too close together, clustering like pomegranate seeds. The smell of licorice floats on the air.

A door bangs shut at the back of the shop, and April turns, startled. Behind the counter, there's nothing but an unbroken wall. No door, and no baristas, either. She's positive there were two baristas behind the counter when she entered the shop, but the space between the counter and the wall is empty. The playful tune has fallen silent.

As she stares, confused and frightened, a door that didn't exist a moment ago opens in the wall. Behind the door, a stairway spirals up at a crazy angle. She sees people going up, people coming down, their faces strangely alight. The people going up diminish as they rise, their bodies shrinking to nothing as if swallowed by a vast distance. The people coming down disperse as they descend, the different parts of them moving along different paths until they're spread through all space, everywhere and nowhere.

There's something wrong with the directions back there. Up and down and near and far are getting tangled. The diagram is turning inside out. It has something to do with the light, with the coffee, with the faces of the people going up and coming down. Faces that look strange, on which the light gleams strangely. Faces too close to the skull, too pale with dim holes, shining with liquid, swirling and rippling like dark water stirred by huge, hidden creatures. Faces almost human, but not quite. As if those people had lost the knack of being human, had been distracted from humanity by the difficulty of moving through that space with its tangled, uncertain directions, its strange light gleaming everywhere.

Two dim, distorted shapes race down the stairs, slip through the door and into the shop. Banging shut, the door ceases to exist. Two baristas stand behind the counter, one beside the cash register and one beside the espresso machine. Their gray aprons bear the shop's logo: a curled-up, sleeping kitten. The thought bubble over the kitten's head holds the name of the shop, which April has never bothered to remember. She prefers to think of it as simply "the coffee shop around the corner," as if there were no other. DREAMLAND COFFEE, the bubble says.

The playful tune has returned to the air, spilling from the puckered mouth of the person beside the espresso machine. The person beside the cash register bobs her head to the tune, light gleaming from something like eyes in something like a face. Radiant holes in a wavering outline.

It's all too much. April wants to leave this awful place, to run home screaming from this horrible nightmare, curl up in bed and close her eyes tight until she falls into an unbroken sleep. But what she does bears no relation to what she wants. It's as if her thoughts and desires are arrayed on the x- and y-axes, clear and logical, while her actions slide down the z-axis into a yawning abyss. As if she's a figure in someone else's diagram, something else's dream. She approaches the counter at the back of the shop.

"Sorry to keep you waiting," says the person beside the register. "Shift change. What can we get you?"

April opens her mouth, but no sound comes out. Terror has her throat in its strangling grip.

"You look like you could use something extra-strong," says the person beside the machine.

April nods. The machine person begins pressing buttons, twisting knobs. A clanking purr rises from the machine, harmonizing with the playful tune.

The register person leans an elbow on the counter. "Awful, isn't it?" she whispers with something like a sympathetic smile, something white and gleaming.

"Yes," April whispers. "It's horrible."

Licorice-scented steam billows from the purring machine. Dark liquid flows into a waiting cup printed with the shop's logo. The machine person slides the cup along the counter toward the register.

"On the house. You look like you could use it," the register person says.

"Thanks." April takes a sip. The coffee is scalding hot, but the heat is painless, as if the nerves that carry discomfort to her brain have been cauterized. Or maybe the heat is so painful that she's gone insane and doesn't know the cup has dropped from her hand, she's fallen to the floor, she's writhing and shrieking in terrible agony. Either way. The coffee slides down her throat, curls up in her stomach.

"Hits the spot, right?" the machine person says. The steam from the machine has condensed in viscous droplets all over his face. Blobs of liquid roll down his cheeks like gluey tears.

The blend isn't April's favorite, but she nods anyway. The extra-strong coffee is spiraling outward from her stomach into the rest of her, licorice-scented tendrils tunneling through her flesh.

"You know," the register person says, "you're holding up really well, considering ..."—she waves her hand around—"... everything."

April doesn't know how to respond to that. She takes a long breath, impossibly long and wide, as if the spiraling tendrils have carved a huge void where her lungs used to be. A licorice-scented bubble big enough to hold all the air in the universe.

Deep breath. No. Long, wide. The diagram is in tatters.

April leans forward across the counter. "Can you tell me what's happening?"

The register person smiles. "It's all coming together," she says. The machine person nods, the liquid rippling across his face.

April takes a deep breath. "About that sign on the door ..."

The register person interrupts her. "Looks like someone's here for you," she says, pointing a tall finger over April's shoulder.

April turns. It's Evan, standing in the middle of the shop. The strange light gleams so brightly behind him that nothing outside can be seen, no street, no buildings, no sky. Evan holds a cup with a kitten printed on it, curled up and dreaming of a name April doesn't recognize: NIGHTMARE COFFEE.

Seeing Evan at last, April doesn't feel much. A little annoyance, a little curiosity. She knows she used to have other feelings about him, strong, rich, complex feelings, but she can't remember what they were. The tendrils have carved all that away.

Cup in hand, annoyed and curious, she approaches him. "Since when is there another coffee shop around the corner?" she says.

Evan shrugs. "A new place just opened up. Thought I'd give it a try."

"And why did you ask me to come meet you? Why didn't you just come back to the apartment? It's awful out here. It's horrible."

"I know. I wanted to go back. I tried. But I just ..." He shakes his head, his eyes bleary with confusion. "It didn't happen like I wanted." Evan's face looks stranger than ever, so tight against the skull it's practically splitting open, spilling another face through the cracks. His eyebrows glisten and twitch like antennae picking up the whispers in the air, the playful tune.

April sighs. "Whatever. How's the coffee?"

"Have a taste."

She takes Evan's cup and sips. Nutmeg-scented, much better than what's in her own cup.

"It's good," she says.

"Yeah, it's all right. But I think I prefer the coffee here, actually. Wanna switch?"

Another foolish request. Classic Evan. But what does it matter now? She gives him her cup, takes his.

"They're hiring baristas here," she says.

Evan snorts. "Again with this. Why on earth would you want to work at a coffee shop? You have a Ph.D.!"

April sighs. "At this point, I'll take anything. And my Ph.D. is absolutely meaningless." She's said it before, almost believed it. Now, she knows it's true. She takes a sip from Evan's cup.

As she drinks the coffee from the other shop, nutmeg-scented tendrils spiral through her. They tangle with the licorice-scented tendrils, twisting and folding the space those tendrils carved until the void is writhing, flexing, pushing against her flesh from the inside. She raises a hand to her cheek. Moist, viscous skin ripples against her fingertips.

"Hey," she says. "Do I look ... strange?"

Evan smiles or scowls, she can't tell which and doesn't care. "I wasn't going to say anything," he says. His voice sounds dry, raspy.

Evan's smile or scowl suddenly fades. He cocks his head like he's listening for something, trying to decide if a sound he's hearing is real or just his imagination. After a moment, April hears it, too: a purr, deeper than the purr of the espresso machine. As the purr grows louder, Evan's eyes widen. His lips peel back from his teeth. April's never seen anyone look so terrified.

"It's happening again," he says, his voice crumbling. He points a desiccated finger over April's shoulder.

April turns toward the back of the shop. The door stands open, the stairway spiraling up at a crazy angle behind it. Clouds of oily steam glint rainbows around the stairs, swirling and pulsing to the purr's deafening rhythm. The register person is climbing, removing her gray apron as the distance swallows her. The machine person, his foot on the first stair, beckons to April with a movement of his shining head.

No, April thinks. *No. No. No.*

But the diagram says otherwise. She strides like a figment of something else's imagination along the z-axis toward the open door. The void twists and folds inside her, forming whirlpools in her flesh. The monstrous purr blends with the whispers that still fill the shop, though the people are no longer leaning together over the tables but rising to watch April as she approaches the door, the clusters of heads scattering like seeds that crunch under her feet.

Another set of footsteps crunches behind her. She supposes Evan is following her toward the back of the shop, the diagram sliding him, too, in an unthought, unwanted direction.

Behind the door, the machine person grins. He holds out a dripping hand, a set of gray coveralls dangling from his fingers. Pointless thoughts swarm in April's mind as she nears the threshold, questions whirling in the void like shredded stars around a black hole. *What's happening? Where am I going? Why did I come here? Why me?* Clear, logical, pointless, gleaming strangely in the abyss as she slips through the door, puts on the coveralls, and assumes the duties of a position whose nature she'll never manage to unravel unless it's in a dream she won't remember, her own nightmare or something else's.

How I Turned My Little Brother Human

When the air went bad, everyone fell asleep except mama and me.

For a while it was just us two, drinking the river, eating whatever came up. Nice, quiet. Then mama said she had another me in her tummy.

"I don't know how it happened," she said. "A miracle from God." I never met God but mama always said how he gave us miracles, the sun and stars and all.

Mama's tummy grew and grew. I brought her river water when her head got hot.

One day mama screamed and I got so scared I fell down. When I got up, mama was asleep and my little brother was born. He wasn't human yet. Just a lump, no arms or legs or nothing, lying all gray and bloody on the floor.

I rolled him to the river and cleaned him up. I stuck in sticks for arms and legs, black stones for eyes, white stones for teeth. Green leaves for hair, red flowers for lips.

I took him back home and sat him in a chair next to mama. "Look, mama," I said, "a miracle. Our baby's human now."

"Buzz buzz," said the flies on her lips. What I think that means is, "Thank you, sweetheart."

The German Cousin

Cousinship had limits but no one knew enough to fix them.
- Henry Adams

ISMENE. Was ist's, du scheinst ein rotes Wort zu färben?
- Friedrich Hölderlin

<u>1. Zimmerlausch</u>

From my bedroom, the sound could be anything. A chorus of sobs, birds' babble in the yard, pots and pans clattering in the kitchen. I set my book on the bed, its black cover obscuring the comforter's flowers, and rise to investigate.

My bare feet scuff in the hallway. Through the open door to the twins' room, I see a tangle of video game controllers, muscled figures paused in mid-fight on the television. In Hilda's room, stuffed animals and crayons lie scattered across the floor. The guest room door is closed, our guest's white slippers gone from their place at the threshold. No one here.

The living room curtains are drawn, the lamps off. On the floorboards, a haze of light stretches away from my feet, narrowing to a bright blade where the basement door stands ajar. The sound rises from below, clearer now: laughter. The children and our guest, my dead husband's cousin Sophie, are down in the rec room, playing a game.

I sigh, relieved. No one has laughed in this house for a long time.

Returning to bed, I pause outside the guest room. Did I hear a sound from behind the door? Another laugh, or something else this time, a sob, a bird? I linger, listening. Nothing. I continue along the hallway, reflecting how the ear plays us false. It deceives. That is just the word—"deceives."

Sitting on the bed, reaching for my book, I wonder how to say "deceives" in German. In the days since Cousin Sophie arrived on our doorstep, the sticker on her white suitcase proclaiming FRA for Frankfurt Airport, I've been picking up bits of German, words and phrases here and there. Sophie crossed an ocean to join us in our time of sorrow, and I'd like to repay her kindness by crossing the waves of language. Her English is excellent, but her voice carries a sad undertone when she speaks it. She sounds lonely and lost, the tongue in her mouth not her own.

I take my phone from the bedside table, open the translation app and type, "The ear deceives." After a moment, the app responds, "*Das Ohr täuscht.*" My lips move silently, savoring the umlaut.

That is exactly what the ear does. "Deceives" was wrong. The ear *täuscht*, precisely.

<u>2. Zauberspruch</u>

When I wake from my nap, the house smells delicious. Roast beef, potatoes, herbs and spices. In the dining room, the children and our guest greet me with smiles, Tristan and Caroline on one side of the table, Hilda and Cousin Sophie on the other. Serving dishes crowd the middle of the table, but the children's plates are empty, their silverware lying prim and straight. Sophie has no plate in front of her.

"I hope you haven't been waiting long," I say. "I was just so tired."

"Not at all," Sophie says. Her vowels are round, her consonants throaty. She sets a hand on Hilda's shoulder, her white-painted nails bright against the girl's pink shirt. "This sweet one wanted to rouse you, but I said no, let your mother sleep."

The twins pull the dish of roast beef toward their side of the table. I reach for the dish of potatoes. "Well, you certainly didn't need to stand on ceremony. You must be hungry after all the fun you had earlier. I heard you chortling in the basement."

Sophie says, "Pardon me, but what is 'chortling'?"

I smile sheepishly. "I'm sorry. That's a silly word to use. It's like laughing, but ..." My mind goes blank. What is "chortling"? "Kids, help me out. Who knows how to chortle?"

Caroline chortles theatrically, "Hoo, hoo, hoo." Tristan snorts in derision, Caroline slaps his shoulder, and Tristan's eyes go furious. He wheels toward his twin, a beast's snarl on his lips.

"Children," Sophie says. "*Seid nicht böse.*"

Ducking their heads in apology, the twins return to their meat.

Sophie says, "I like this chortling. Where I live, we might say *glucksen* or *jauchzen.*"

I take my phone from my pocket, open the notes app. "Would you mind writing those down for me? I want some happy words in my vocabulary." I slide the phone toward Sophie. "And could you also write out what you said to the twins? It worked like a charm. They never stop fighting when I ask them to."

"We weren't fighting," Tristan mumbles around a mouthful of flesh.

I skewer a chunk of potato and slide it into my mouth. Starch and salt and dill and vinegar, all bedded in warm, dark earth. The flavors whirl in my head, whirl my thoughts back to the days when William would make dinner every evening, before his mind began twisting in on itself, corroding. He cooked pork chops, dumplings, cabbage, potatoes—exactly these potatoes. I close my eyes, stop chewing. Holding the crushed mass on my tongue, I question the taste, measure it against the one in my memory. A true, perfect recreation. A resurrection.

When I open my eyes, tears spill out. My phone lies in front of me, white-nailed fingers sliding from its black surface. Cousin Sophie's lips tighten with concern. "Are you well, dear one?"

I swallow, brush the tears away. "I'm fine, it's just ... William used to make these potatoes."

She nods. "A family recipe. We cousins learned the art together in our grandmother's kitchen, a swarm of children around her knees as she taught us the steps, the ingredients." Sophie's face is illuminated, her pale eyes piercing through time. "I see the old woman now, her hands *knorrig wie Wurzeln*—knotted, gnarled as roots—holding things up, naming them. A potato: '*Kartoffel*!' A bottle of vinegar: '*Essig*!' She was a great teacher, and *Vetter Wilhelm*—Cousin William—he and I were her most precious pupils. Oh, poor William, *armer Vetterling* ..."

I wipe fresh tears from my eyes. Hilda's face crumples, disappears into the crook of her arm. Sophie strokes Hilda's trembling back, murmuring, "*Sei rühig*, sweet one, he lives in our heart, he is with us still ..."

Across the table, the twins keep eating, piling their plates with food. Their eyes scan the tableau of grief with cold detachment, their lips smirking between forkfuls. They're evil. I hate them.

I gasp at my own unbidden, sickening thoughts. My stomach churns. Sickening thoughts, precisely. I lurch to my feet. "I'm sorry, I need to ..." I rush from the room, clamping a hand over my mouth to dam the vomit.

Hilda wails behind me as I run to the hallway, the bathroom. Her cries of "Mama, Mama" drift through the door, weaving among the sounds of retching and splashing as I empty myself of everything. Potatoes rise acid-drenched from the tomb of my stomach to burn my throat and sully my tongue, and in losing the meal I lose William again, he bursts away from me in shuddering waves, he will not stay.

I rest my cheek against the cool porcelain. I can barely restrain myself from scooping the sludge from the bowl, forcing William back into me. Instead, I watch the mess as it wheels slowly, the heavy bits settling. I think of William's face at the front door, the smile that flashed across it when I turned back in the driveway. Hilda yanking fruitlessly at the car door, the twins swinging their backpacks at each other. William's hand rising, the keys dangling from his fingers. When I ran back to snatch the keys, his lips swooped to brush my cheek, and his smile said, *Don't be afraid. Together, we'll beat this thing.*

William's smile, and the ruin I found in the bedroom when I came home, the awful horror, swirl of dark clots around a form slumped heavily against the wall with a gun in its lap. Heavy bits settling. The eye deceives, the heart. You played me false, love.

I stare into the bowl. The bits swirl. *Kartoffel. Essig.* I flush, lie down on the tiles, close my eyes. I sink in the honest dark.

Rising is harder than lying down. My knees crack as I stand. I rinse my mouth, wash my face, smile into the mirror. *Täuschend.*

My emptied stomach growls for a second chance. I head for the dining room, past the closed doors of the hallway. From the twins' room, I hear cartoonish kicks and punches, curses and inhuman grunts as Tristan and Caroline brutalize each other's avatars. From Hilda's room, sobs and murmurs, our guest soothing the heart-stricken child with gentle words. Giving comfort, just as she said she'd do when she offered to come stay with us.

Passing the guest room, I glance downward. I freeze.

White slippers on the threshold.

If Cousin Sophie is in Hilda's room, what are her slippers doing here? She never leaves the guest room without them. If the slippers are on the threshold, she's in the room; if not, she's not. My heart pounds as I realize how much I've come to depend on that regularity. If she's left the room without taking her slippers, if she's done so even once, what can I rely on? Anything might be anywhere at any time. Anything might happen.

I remember her voice over the phone, saying she'd cross the ocean to help us, to steady our shipwrecked lives. "I will cook meals. I will bring games and stories for the children. You have suffered. My poor cousin has left you suffering. Let me be a comfort to you." Some comfort. I gaze bitterly down at the slippers.

Behind the guest room door, a voice speaks softly. I can't make out the words, but it's the same voice I just heard in my memory, Sophie's voice gone out of my head and through the door. Nothing will stay in its place. I start to shiver.

A second voice mutters from the guest room, deeper than the first. My ears strain for words but hear only sounds, swirling bits of obscured language that might mean anything at all. The voices speak in turn, the incomprehensible sounds echoing, as if the second voice is repeating after the first.

The second voice falters, breaks into quiet laughter. Chortling. William's smile flashes in my memory, a wild surmise out of nowhere. My heart goes numb. My shaking hand flies to the doorknob.

The room is dim, lit only by the evening light through the window. No one there, no voices. At the foot of the bed, Sophie's white suitcase lies closed.

I step backward into the hallway, perplexed. I glance down at the threshold. No slippers.

My breath comes in tattered gasps. What's German for "I'm going insane"? My phone is in the dining room. I must not lose control, must retain my hold on what's true. My phone is in the dining room. My dead husband is not in the guest room. No slippers are on the threshold. I put one foot in front of the other, left foot then right foot, a perfect regularity.

Serving dishes on the dining room table. Half-laden plates, dirty silverware. No phone.

I grasp the back of a chair to keep from falling. Who could have stolen my phone away? Who would do such a thing? Not sweet Hilda, so sensitive and loving. Not Cousin Sophie, who crossed an ocean to bring comfort, to save me from suffering.

The twins' faces twist in my mind. Smirking, mocking, evil.

I stumble back down the hallway, past the white slippers, past the sobs and murmurs from Hilda's room, the twins' bestial noises. No point confronting them tonight, when I'm so tired and empty, devoid even of hunger. I shut the bedroom door behind me, click on the light.

On the comforter, hiding the flowers, two black rectangles. The glossy cover of my book, the shiny screen of my phone.

Everything deceives. The ear, the heart, the mind, *alles täuscht.*

I unlock the phone. The notes app is open, the words and phrases I'd asked about dutifully listed. *Glucksen. Jauchzen. Seid nicht böse.*

I open the translation app and type, "I'm going insane." "*Ich werde verrückt,*" the app responds. That's exactly what I'm doing. *Ich werde verrückt.*

Flipping the settings for source and destination, I type, "*Seid nicht böse.*" The app responds, "Don't be cross." I delete "*Seid nicht.*" By itself, "*böse*" calls up many results—"angry," "wicked," "vicious," "naughty," "nasty," on and on, a haze of words narrowing toward a meaning.

The twins aren't "evil" after all, not precisely. They're *böse.*

———◆———

3. Zuckergeld

I lie sleepless in the dark, words swirling and settling in my mind. What does the heart do? *Täuscht.* What am I going? *Verrückt.* What are the twins? *Böse.* What is coming? *Gericht.*

What was that last one? I sit up in bed to check the translation app, but before I can unlock my phone, sounds from the hallway distract me. The swish of a door, shuffling footsteps on the floorboards.

I rise, slip silently out of my bedroom and down the hallway. The guest room threshold is vacant, slipperless. No one in the living room, the basement door closed. Through the dining room, from the kitchen, a warm light shines, gleaming on the table's empty slab.

I stand in the entryway of the kitchen. On the stove, blue flames flicker beneath a saucepan. Swathed in a white night-gown, Sophie stares into the pan, muttering under her breath. She acknowledges my presence with the briefest of glances, turns her eyes back to the stove.

The kitchen counter is spotless, the sink empty of dishes, the linoleum freshly mopped. Our guest is a good housekeeper, better than I could be. Keeping things tidy was William's job, and when he couldn't do it anymore, I knew things had gone badly wrong. Nothing was in its place.

Seeing the kitchen so neat and clean, I feel my heart swell with gratitude. Cousin Sophie has done so much for us. In so many little ways, she's brought William back. I wish I could do something to repay her.

A rattling rises from the saucepan as its contents begin to boil. Sophie turns to me. "Dear one, would you fetch me the sugar?"

The sugar is where it should be, in a tall canister by the sink. I bring it over to the stove. "Do you need a tablespoon? A measuring cup?"

"No." She dips her hand into the canister, dumps a glittering palmful into the saucepan, her white nails flashing above the water. At the bottom of the pan, beneath the spreading sugar-cloud, something gleams. "You see, I go by feeling, by the heart."

"*Das Herz täuscht,*" I say.

She gives me a rueful smile. "Just so, dear one. It is good to hear the truth spoken in my own tongue."

As the sugar dissolves, the gleam below comes into focus. A gold coin lies submerged in the pan, flipping over and over in the roiling water.

"A trick of my grandmother," Sophie says. "A balm for the unsleeping. When we cousins would lie awake, the old woman's lessons turning, twisting, whirling in our brains until we cried out for terror and wonder, nothing but this treat could quiet us. And when little *Vetter Wilhelm* left us, when his parents took him away across the ocean, again I lay restless and cried out, fearing what might befall him so far from home."

She turns back to the stove, lowers the flame. As the water cools, the spinning coin slows, and soon I can make out the images it bears. The coin is double-headed, a golden face in profile on each side, but where one face is sharply limned, its heroic features and resolute eye as clear as if minted yesterday, the other face is worn and faded, its contours dulled as though a billion thumbs had rubbed across it. The ruin of a face, a face turning not-face.

Sophie points a white-nailed finger into the water. "A present from the old woman. When the time came for me to go out from her kitchen, she pressed it into my palm and said, 'For as long as you live, dear one, this coin will spin, showing now one side and now another, so that not until you draw your last breath will the true face of your life be revealed.' Such was her gift to each of us cousins as we left to find our way. *Vetter Wilhelm* had his bequest, too, his token of true and false faces."

The coin blurs in my vision. My voice shakes. "He never told me about it. I didn't know about any of this. William hated talking about his childhood."

"Well, one does not speak of such things to strangers."

The word pierces my heart, hollows it. I stagger backward, away, but Sophie rushes toward me, folds me in her white-swathed arms and murmurs in my ear, "Oh, dear one, that is not what I meant! Damn this lying English, this false tongue. *Ausländer*, that is the word, not 'stranger.' Forgive my blunder. I know *Vetter Wilhelm* loved you most deeply."

I sob on her shoulder, my tears wetting her nightgown. "Then why didn't he trust me? Why didn't he tell me the truth?"

She holds me tighter. "He never knew how! His parents snatched him away too early, carried him across the ocean before our grandmother's teaching was done. He never grasped the structure of our language, the truth of its syntax; he'd learned only a rubbish of words, neither true nor false, a birdish *Gezwitscher* of syllables. How could he tell you a truth he never knew? And how could he ever know it, stolen away to this land of falsehood, a lying tongue of English stuffed in his mouth? But fret not, dear one. I have come to set things right, to put things in their places."

The strength goes out of me. I sag against her like an empty sack. "I don't understand," I moan. "I don't understand."

"You will," she murmurs.

Breathing deep, I collect myself while Sophie takes the saucepan from the stove. Water sloshes in the sink. Metal clinks in the pan. She comes to me with her hand held out, her slippers swishing on the linoleum.

"I meant this for myself," she says, "but I see your need is greater. Open your mouth."

Gold shines against her palm's pale flesh. Uncomprehending, I stare at the ruin, the not-face.

She points at her mouth. "*Öffne deinen Mund.*"

I open my mouth.

"Now, be calm, *Liebchen, sei rühig.*"

I stand utterly still as she places the sugared coin on my tongue. Sweetness and bitterness flood through me, more intense than anything I've ever tasted, and without thinking, I close my lips, take the ruin into me. The metal carves a path of cold fire down my throat.

Realizing what I've done, I flush with shame. "Your grandmother's gift ... I'm so sorry ..."

"Not at all." Sophie reaches into the folds of her nightgown. A coin gleams between her fingers. She smiles. "*Die Zunge täuscht.* The tongue, the heart, and all." Her hand cups my cheek. "You will rest now, dear one, while I stay here a moment to tidy up. Soon things will be clearer. *Gute Nacht.*" She turns away, goes to the sink. Water gurgles in the drain.

Fatigue washes over me, pulls me down toward endless depths of sleep. I drift through the dining room, down the hallway, past the closed doors. I see a white blur in the darkness, white slippers on a threshold, hear whispers from a room, the twins' room, and in swirling depths I glimpse a figure bent over a bed, its face hideous, destroyed, from the shattered not-mouth drop chirps and trills that plunge unmeaning into wicked ears, *böse Ohren*, but everything melts away in the tide of sleep, even terror is only a slow drifting. Shaking faintly, delirious in the drift of terror and exhaustion, I stumble into my bedroom, sprawl on the comforter, feel a cold shape beneath me as I drift further and further, a cold black shape, a book, a phone, *täuschend, verrückt*, words and translations, corroded black coins of truth.

---

4. Zorngericht

Creak, creak. The door inches open. Hilda's face peeks shyly through the gap. "Mama, are you awake?"

The room is golden with sun. I yawn and stretch, my limbs twisting beneath the comforter's flowers. "Yes, honey. What time is it? Have you had breakfast?"

"It's noon. Cousin Sophie made porridge, and I helped. Now we're making lunch. She's teaching me how to cook."

"That's very nice of her." My hand slips under the pillow, finds something hard and smooth. Book or phone? "Tell Cousin Sophie I'll be right there."

"Okay, Mama."

The scuff of her bare feet on the floorboards goes straight to my heart. How could William have doubted this unmistakable world we'd made together? How could he have wanted to leave it?

Rising, I reach under the pillow to pull out the hard, smooth thing. Not a book or a phone but a tablet, a black e-reader. I could have sworn I had a book or a phone. Both? Neither. With a flick of my wrist, I send the tablet spinning onto the comforter. It darkens the flowers.

All the doors along the hallway are open. I pass Hilda's room with its stuffed animals and crayons, the twins' room with its tangled controllers, its frenzied, immobilized effigies. In the guest room, at the foot of the bed, a white suitcase lies closed.

The suitcase shakes, thumps against the bed frame.

I freeze in the doorway, staring. My heart quails as sounds rise from the suitcase, a scrabble and a sob and a broken, desolate mutter. The voice is deep, its rhythm halting, its words not words at all but a chattering chaos, the babble of someone who never learned to speak.

Fingers scratch against the inside of the suitcase. "Varr," the voice says. "Tersta, corlech. Helk. Varr."

I tremble on the threshold. The suitcase lurches, its silver clasps rattling on the floor. For a moment, I long to undo the clasps, but my mind recoils. What desperate fingers would clutch mine, what ruined not-face peer out at me? *"Das Ohr täuscht, das Ohr täuscht,*" I whisper, but I know there's no deception here, only sheerest truth. Unmistakable, unbearable.

The voice growls like a beast, low and guttural. "Varr. Varr."

No, not "Varr. Varr." "*Wahr. Wahr.*" True, true, true ...

I wrench myself away from the guest room, run down the hallway, through the dining room. In the kitchen, Hilda is crouching in front of the oven, peering through the dark glass.

I take a deep breath. "Honey, where's Cousin Sophie?" Horror frays the edges of my voice.

Hilda turns toward me. She's wearing a white apron, a child-sized chef's hat. "We were making lunch, but Tristan and Caroline were being naughty, so Cousin Sophie took them to the basement to play a game. She told me to watch the potatoes while she's gone." Looking up at me, she frowns, her kind eyes widening. "Are you okay, Mama?"

I try to smile. "I'm fine. I just need to talk to Cousin Sophie."

The basement door is ajar. Light shines from below. As I descend, laughter rises to meet me.

In the rec room, Sophie sits cross-legged on the couch, robed in a blanket from the linen closet. The twins kneel on the carpet in front of her, clasping their hands to their chests as if pleading for mercy. All three of them are laughing. My heart races as I hesitate at the bottom of the stairs.

Sophie turns to me with a smile, beckons me toward the couch. "We are playing *Gericht*, the game of judgment," she says. "These naughty children have come before the court to hear their sentence. The verdict is imminent, but I'm afraid I must return upstairs to make sure sweet Hilda does not burn the potatoes. Dear one, will you mount the seat of justice in my place? I know you will judge rightly."

"In your room ..." I stammer. "Your suitcase ... I heard ..."

She nods. "Just so. What you heard is of great concern to you, and we will discuss it fully. But justice cannot wait." She rises from the couch, pats the cushion with white-nailed fingers. "Please sit. You will do me this favor, *nicht wahr*?"

Shining with certainty, her pale eyes hold my gaze. She's done so much, helped me in so many ways; how can I refuse her? I sit on the couch. She wraps the blanket around my shoulders.

Kneeling before me, Tristan and Caroline smirk and roll their eyes in derision. Tristan unclasps his hands just long enough to swat Caroline's shoulder. Caroline returns the blow. They squirm, they groan, they chortle.

I stare at their faces, so similar yet not the same, two sides of a spinning coin. Divided like truth and falsehood, playing at war with each other, taking nothing seriously. Not even their father's death has humanized them. But how could it have been any different? Born severed, one true and one false, never knowing which was which. A father who never learned to tell the truth, and a mother ...

What kind of mother am I? I think of the voice from the suitcase, its inarticulate babbling. Bad enough to have one parent who can't talk sense, but two? Luckily, I've learned better. I may not have had a grandmother to show me the true path, but at least now I have a cousin.

I raise my hands, the blanket dangling from my arms. I try to maintain my composure, but my voice shakes with righteous fury as I say, "Hear the verdict of justice." The twins stop squirming, squint up at me from the carpet. The mockery fades from their faces.

"I hereby pronounce your nature," I say. "You are naughty, wicked children. *Ihr seid böse.*"

Caroline says, "Mom? Are you okay?"

Pity surges in my heart. My eyes swim with tears. The twins never asked to be what they are. Why not release them from it, pronounce a merciful sentence?

I hold my hands out to the twins in loving entreaty. "*Kinder, seid nicht böse.*"

The sentence is carried out at once. No longer at war, the twins embrace, cling to one another with long-denied affection. Divided no more, the coin stops spinning, the two faces blend into one, flesh flowing, reshaping, truth-forged. When the molten bits settle into place, there are no Tristan and Caroline, no *böse Kinder*, only the good child Tristoline, so obedient and true, the child William and I always wanted.

Tears course down my cheeks. I open my arms. "*Komm zu mir, Kind.*"

Tristoline rises from the carpet, staggers blindly toward me. The child's face is worn and featureless, corroded by truth's furnace blast. No eyes to mock, no mouth to smirk. A muffled sob emerges from the swirl of flesh, a newborn creature's whimper of confusion.

I wrap Tristoline in the comforting folds of my blanket, set the child next to me on the couch. I murmur endearments into the ruin of an ear. The child falls silent, quivering in my arms. After a while, beneath the low hum of my own voice, I hear another sound, like water gurgling in a drain. My stomach is growling.

Only now do I notice the wonderful smell wafting down from above. The feast is about to start. "I love you, sweetheart," I whisper. Leaving the faceless child throned in the seat of justice, I ascend the stairs.

The dining room is empty, the table laden with potatoes, cabbage, dumplings, a loaf of dark bread. I stand in the doorway, drawing the scents deep into my lungs. Saliva fills my mouth, sweet and metallic. A thrill of anticipation runs through me.

Careful—even the nose deceives. But no. *Die Nase täuscht nicht*. I breathe deep, savoring the odor of truth.

A clatter rings from the kitchen. Slippers swish on linoleum. Sophie enters the dining room, stately as a priestess in her white apron and chef's hat. Her arms strain with the weight of the final dish, a huge, steaming roast on a black carving board. I hurry forward to clear a space on the table.

Sophie wipes her hands on her apron. "How goes it down below, dear one? How is the child?"

I smile. "*Das Kind ist gut*. And Hilda? Is she still in the kitchen? I hope she wasn't too much in the way while you were cooking."

"Not at all, dear one." She sighs. "If anything, too much out of the way. I did my best to teach her the art, but she held back, clinging to the familiar, too much in love with her false tongue." She lifts a carving knife from the black board. "I would hold this up, name it: '*Messer*!' And she would shake her head and cry, 'Knife, knife!' Perhaps if I had been a great teacher, with the patience of a saint ... but no." Her eyes glisten. She sets down the knife, brushes away a tear. "A sweet, gentle child, *zärtlich wie Kalbfleisch*—tender as veal. Too tender for truth's bitter mouthful."

Bitter, yes. A pang wrings my heart. Is there any end to loss, to sacrifice? How much more will truth demand of me?

Sophie takes my hand, gives it a commiserating squeeze. I never noticed how knotted her fingers are, gnarled and wizened from a lifetime of setting things right, putting things in their places. I grasp her hand tight like an anchoring root. What else is there to hold on to?

"Help me, Sophie," I say, sobs wrenching my throat. "I don't know what's happening. Please teach me. Help me understand."

She pulls me to her. I weep like a child in her arms. "Dear one, of course I will teach you. You've learned so much already, my precious pupil. You've come to the very threshold. The feast is laid above, the child sits in judgment below. Soon the lost one returns, the one snatched away too early."

"I don't understand," I moan, my voice ragged with sorrow and perplexity. "I don't understand."

Sounds from the back of the house interrupt my sobs. A snap, a thump, a rustle. At first they could be anything, but soon the picture comes clear in my mind. Silver clasps opening. A white lid falling against floorboards. An entombed form emerging, rising unsteadily into the light.

Quaking with terror, I squeeze my eyes shut, press my face into Sophie's shoulder. "*Ich bin verrückt geworden*," I murmur.

She strokes my hair. "*Nein, Liebchen. Sei rühig. Vetter Wilhelm kommt.*"

An arrhythmic shuffling in the hallway. Bare feet on floorboards, the tentative steps of someone trying to remember how to walk, snatching at vague memories swirling in a haze of deception. A guttural voice mutters nonsense. "Varr, falsh, varr ..."

"We must be patient with him," Sophie whispers. "After such long wanderings, it is hard to recall the truth. He will be disoriented, still half-lost in falsehood. And he will be hungry."

The shuffling footsteps enter the living room. Still uncertain, moving in fits and starts, but gaining confidence as the haze recedes. "*Wahr*," the voice mutters. "*Hungrig.*"

My own stomach rumbles. Lifting my head from Sophie's shoulder, I turn to face the table. The feast lies ready, filling the house with its delicious aroma. At the end of my strength, drained by confusion and horror, I seize at the only certainty. I need to eat.

Sophie gives me an understanding smile. "You have suffered much, dear one. *Vetter Wilhelm* will join us in his own time, but we need not stand on ceremony. Let us begin."

Taking the knife from the black carving board, she holds it up to my gaze. "*Messer.*"

"*Messer,*" I repeat.

She points a knotted finger at the steaming roast. "*Fleisch.*"

"*Fleisch.*"

She grips the knife by the blade, extends the handle toward me. "Will you do the honors, *Vetterin*?"

Content Warnings

The Consultant's Hand: child death

Estrangements: mariticide, child death

Exuviae: home invasion

Flesh Advent: abuse of authority, graphic injury to child

A Goodnight Kiss from Aunt Spider: death of animal (spider)

The World of Iniquity Among Our Members Is the Tongue: parent death, verbal abuse

Winter Savory: elder abuse

Osculum: graphic injury

Graceful Degradation: parent death

Smoochfest: dismemberment, nonconsensual touch

How I Turned My Little Brother Human: parent death, death in childbirth

The German Cousin: suicide, harm/threat to children

Acknowledgements

Thanks to my parents and sisters, who not only provided immense love and encouragement but also listened to me read some of these stories aloud on our family Zoom calls. If the horror writer's secret dream is to make their loved ones wince, I'm living the dream.

Thanks to my critique partners at Brooklyn Speculative Fiction Writers, who provided insightful comments on several of these stories and whose feedback benefited even the stories they didn't read. May every writer stumbling toward publication find such a generous and supportive community.

Thanks to the editors who gave many of these stories a first home, and a double dose of thanks to Eric Raglin for his excellent work as this collection's editor and publisher. May a thousand Morsels bloom, each more Cursed than the last.

Thanks to the wonderful writers who provided blurbs, and to Trevor Henderson for the awesome cover art.

Thanks to the weirdo reading this—yes, YOU in particular!

Last and most, thanks to Celina, my favorite person, for years of boundless love and mutual support. This collection is dedicated to her, especially the funny parts.

Publication History

"The Consultant's Hand" was first published in *Bitter Apples* (Cursed Morsels Press, 2023)

"Estrangements" was first published in *The First Five Minutes of the Apocalypse* (Hungry Shadow Press, 2023)

"Exuviae" was first published in *Dark Matter Presents: Monster Lairs* (Dark Matter INK, 2023)

"Bite-Apple" was first published in *Dose of Dread* (Dread Stone Press, 2022)

"Flesh Advent" was first published in *Shredded: A Sports and Fitness Body Horror Anthology* (Cursed Morsels Press, 2022)

"Hydra" was first published in *Dark Moments* (Black Hare Press, 2021)

"The World of Iniquity Among Our Members Is the Tongue" was first published in *No Trouble at All* (Cursed Morsels Press, 2023)

"Osculum" was first published in *Ooze: Little Bursts of Body Horror* (ed. Ruth Anna Evans, 2023)

"Graceful Degradation" was first published in *Annus Horribilis: An Anthology of Horror Set in 2022* (Bag of Bones Press, 2022)

"Wheel of Meat" was first published in *Deadly Drabble Tuesday* (Hungry Shadow Press, 2023)

"Smoochfest" was first published in *The Theatre Phantasmagoria* (Night Terror Novels, 2022)

"How I Turned My Little Brother Human" was first published in *206 Word Stories* (Bag of Bones Press, 2022)

About the Author

D. Matthew Urban hails from Texas and lives in Queens, NY, where he reads weird books, watches weird movies, and writes weird fiction. His stories have appeared in *Cosmic Horror Monthly*, *Tales from Between*, and *Fraidy Cat Quarterly*, among other venues, and his novelette "Nonsense Words" was published in *Split Scream 4* by Tenebrous Press. *Shaky Pictures of Vanished Faces* is his first collection. Find him on Twitter/Bluesky @breathinghead or on the web at https://dmatthewurban.com.

Other Books from Cursed Morsels Press

Lupus in Fabula
by Briar Ripley Page

Lupus In Fabula collects thirteen stories about the interplay of lust, violence, yearning, and grief; about becoming a monster and loving monsters; about transformation; about strange occurrences in sad, mundane lives. Whether you prefer witches and werewolves, grisly body horror, or surreal scenes of small town decay, this collection offers something to sink your fangs into.

The Nightmare Box and Other Stories
by Cynthia Gómez

A young queer man finds love at a magical clothing shop—and the courage to stand up to the homophobic cops. A witch who makes custom nightmares wonders why all her victims are connected to the Black Panthers—and who she's really working for. A soon-to-be father encounters a mysterious hitchhiker who tries pulling him back to the days of his violent past. A brand-new vampire, freshly hired at the blood bank, delights in her heightened sexual desire and superhuman strength.

Cynthia Gómez's debut collection is a magic-soaked love letter to Oakland, brimming with feminist rage. Its twelve stories center ordinary people—Latine, queer, working class-as they wield supernatural powers against oppression, loneliness, and dread.

Why Didn't You Just Leave
edited by Julia Rios and Nadia Bulkin

It's the question asked of any story about a haunting: *why didn't you just leave?* But if accounts of people who have stayed in haunted houses are any indication ... it's never that simple.

In this book, you'll find twenty-two all-new stories about the reasons people *don't* leave scary situations—parents who stay in haunted houses to protect their children, convicts who literally can't leave their prison, retail workers who need a paycheck even if it's from a haunted workplace, trauma survivors suffering from agoraphobia, and more.

Featuring Shauntae Ball, I.S. Belle, Die Booth, Max Booth III, Christa Carmen, Raquel Castro, Alberto Chimal, Gabe Converse, Lyndsey Croal, Victoria Dalpe, Alexis DuBon, Corey Farrenkopf, Cassandra Khaw, Joe Koch, E.M. Linden, Steve Loiaconi, R. Diego Martinez, J.A.W. McCarthy, Suzan Palumbo, Tonia Ransom, Rhiannon Rasmussen, and Eden Royce. With illustrations by Luke Spooner, Yves Tourigny, and Yornelys Zambrano.

No Trouble at All
edited by Alexis DuBon and Eric Raglin

Politeness is the glue that holds society together. We are all expected to do our part—a pressure ripe with horror. Rotten, even. Whether we adhere to this contract or defy it, there are consequences. These fifteen stories respond to promises made for us, promises of compliance that cost too much to keep.Fea turing Nadia Bulkin, Shenoa Carroll-Bradd, Ariel Marken Jack, Gwendolyn Kiste, Avra Margariti, J.A.W. McCarthy, R.L Meza, Marisca Pichette, J. Rohr, Simone le Roux, Angela Sylvaine, Nadine Aurora Tabing, Sara Tantlinger, D. Matthew Urban, and Gordon B. White.

Bitter Apples
edited by Eric Raglin

Cursed Morsels Press presents tales of teacher horror from Corey Farrenkopf, Emma E. Murray, Cynthia Gómez, Christi Nogle, D. Matthew Urban, Eric Raglin, and Aurelius Raines II. These writers have worked in the profession, and while their stories are fictional, the darkness they explore is all too real.

In *Bitter Apples*, you'll find students' ghosts haunting classrooms, desperate teachers joining cults, zombies plaguing underfunded schools, and more. The institution of education is rotting. How will we survive its horrors?

Shredded: A Sports and Fitness Body Horror Anthology
edited by Eric Raglin

Reader beware! This sports and fitness body horror anthology is dangerous. Side effects include monstrous steroid transformation, concussion-induced madness, possession by jock ghost, death by yoga cult, and more. Read with caution!

Featuring seventeen reps of terror by Nikki R. Leigh, Tim Meyer, Brandon Applegate, Red Lagoe, Caias Ward, RW DeFaoite, Mae Murray, D. Matthew Urban, Charles Austin Muir, Joe Koch, Michael Tichy, Rien Gray, Robbie Burkhart, Eric Raglin, Matthew Pritt, Madeleine Sardina, Alexis DuBon, and J.A.W. McCarthy.

Antifa Splatterpunk
edited by Eric Raglin

Fascism didn't die in 1945. Its grave was only temporary. Rising again, this undead ideology shambles into the present, gathering power and spreading destruction wherever it goes.

This monster stalks the pages of *Antifa Splatterpunk*, in which sixteen horror writers explore fascism's many terrors: police wielding strange bioweapons against the public, white supremacists annihilating their enemies through dark magic, and TV personalities vilifying all who defy the rising fascist tide.

But these stories are resistance: Nazi-killing demons, Confederate-slaying witches, and everyday people punching fascists in the teeth. Among the gore is a glimmer of hope that one day this monster will return to its grave and never rise again.